stunt

Claudia Dey

Coach House Books | Toronto

Lyrics from 'Hit Me with Your Best Shot,' written by Eddie Schwartz, used by permission. All rights administered by Sony/ATV Music Publishing Canada (SOCAN).

Lyrics from 'Angel of the Morning' by Chip Taylor © 1967 (renewed 1995) EMI Blackwood Music Inc. All rights reserved, international copyright secured. Used by permission.

Canada Council for the Arts	Conseil des Arts du Canada	ONTARIO ARTS COUNCIL CONSEIL DES ARTS DE L'ONTARIO	Canada

Published with the generous assistance of the Canada Council for the Arts and the Ontario Arts Council. Coach House Books also acknowledges the support of the Government of Ontario through the Ontario Book Publishing Tax Credit and the Government of Canada through the Book Publishing Industry Development Program.

LIBRARY AND ARCHIVES CANADA CATALOGUING IN PUBLICATION

Dey, Claudia
    Stunt / Claudia Dey.

ISBN 978-1-55245-195-3

    I. Title.

PS8557.E97S78 2008   C813'.6   C2008-901892-3

for Donald Ian Kerr

*'And the red sun of desire and decision
(the two things that create a live world)
rose higher and higher.'*

Vladimir Nabokov, Lolita

one

It's night. The dead centre of it, bull's-eye black. We're sitting in the wet sand on the shores of Lake Ontario, after riding your bicycle here: you, the pedaller, and me, the pedalled, curled on your handlebars, knees to my chin, eyes fixed on yours. We arrowed south, a perfect downhill, and with a sharp left, stomachs pulled into hard wedges, we sped east onto the straight and narrow of Lake Shore, under the bridges that jackknife it, to this spot. Crabs on pointe. Red ants. Boaters' lost rings. We are father and daughter, fishing on the shores of a radioactive lake. I'm nine. Not sure how old you are. Don't know the day you were born. Only that it was winter. And that it was during a snow-storm, a murderous one.

This night, the weather is terrible. Cold and raining. Unlikely fishing weather. The city asleep behind its great wing. 'We should have brought slickers,' you say and sidle into me. Nightgown soaked and stuck to my skin, I shrug. I am Sancho Panza. 'I like it.' I do a cartwheel for you, legs quick shudders over the moon. You grin smoke.

We've spent every night here for a year, tucked in amongst the boulders. We've never caught anything, not even a shoe, but this doesn't seem to be the point.

Fishing hook held hard in one hand, worm and cigarette in the other, you pass the worm along knuckles until it hangs from your fifth finger. The lake inches up to your high-grade-leather cowboy boots. Size thirteen. Licked with paint. The worm fans its body in the air. Everything instantly lashes and undulations for you, everything instantly mistress. Pink and brown rings contracting, it arches back. It eyes its killer: a man tall as a weather vane. Pinstripe suit, frayed at the cuffs, split and resewed, beard in patches, and a moustache waxed to flatline. Remnants of a handsome man.

Cigarette to your mouth, the stub of your smoke is pulled in, a deep draw, and then pinched between a graveyard of blackening teeth. Never an exhalation. You keep it all. Your lungs: stingrays. Winging out. Eternal.

You puncture the worm.

I hear the worm's death cry. And then rapture, worm rapture, rapture in the death hands of Sheb Wooly Ledoux, worm killer, unflinching man, my father.

You dip your line — twelve feet of household string tied to a straight sapling, small rock for a sinker, safety pin bent for a hook — into the lake. 'It is about the bold statements, my darlin'.' You wrap your arm almost double around me. 'The bold statements.' You peer out at the water. Cross-hatching around your eyes, your face made tributaries by the rain — you are cut from rock. From that original band of granite. The collision, the fire to the air, the melting, the near settling, this is what made you.

The hungry whine of a seagull. The green smell of the lake. No bites.

Suddenly called to attention, you stand, a gazelle full of broken bones. You cover my ears. An explosion across the lake stacks itself up the sky in blacks and reds, bruises and sores. The earth shakes below us. The lake swells and boils in an angry moan. Fish fly out of the water and onto the sand, flipping on their bellies, their backs, trick fish balancing on their tails. Five of them hop neatly into your suit pockets, enough for breakfast. You uncover my ears. You look at me. Your cigarette somehow still lit.

Love me. I dangle these words in front of you like beads on a fine string. *Love me.*

You stroke my hair, cold and slicked. You stroke my face. Thumbs smudging rain. Your hand comes to rest on the back of my neck. I lean in against it.

'We're the same.' I read your lips. Won't get my hearing back until morning.

I close my eyes and smell you in: unwashed man skin, old smoke, cat, wet wool, apple. I reach out in the dark, knowing the path by heart, touch my finger to your mouth, your lips so soft behind the bristle, batter and silk. They open for a second. For the first time, my fingertip allowed to disappear.

The next morning, sand in my sheets:
kippers fanned out – a peacock on the breakfast table,
the taste of metal in my mouth,
you are gone.

You leave behind a note. This one, this last one: a drawing of
a flying monk with an enormous penis and below, in your
exaggerated scrawl, always lower case,

gone to save the world
sorry mink,
immaculata,
sorry
yours
sheb wooly ledoux
asshole

No Eugenia. No Eugenia. None.

I am sitting on our front stoop now. It is the first day. The first day of Sheb Departed. June 7, 1981. Time suspended. For me. Not for the rest of the world. The rest of the world is busy, birds flying through the spokes of a spinning wheel.

Trucks speed along our narrow street swiping side mirrors, Eritrean music pounding and keening, kittens scampering for their brief lives. People holler to each other from open windows. Instructions and promises and *don't forgets*. Milk! Marriage! Go! After the rain last night, the sidewalk is washed clean, cars licked and glinting like the backs of otters. And me. Teeth brushed. Hair brushed. I am ready. Knowing that you did not put me in the note because you mean to take me. Of all the things we agreed upon in silence, this is the biggest.

I wear my black corduroy dress. It will stand up to any weather, wherever you might want to squire me to, whatever clime. I have sewn provisions into the hem: nuts, a handkerchief, rope, a pen and paper and a knife. I will move with you as seamlessly as you move through the world. I will be your shadow.

The twins from next door race by. They are playing Horse and Master in matching brown leotards and tap shoes. They have numbers pinned to their backs, hair in buns, like second heads. They have just come home from a dance competition. I can never tell them apart. They are my age. Their names rhyme. They take turns being mean.

The twins' mother comes from the Perfect Mother Kit. Our mother, Mink, dared us to find her pulse. Mrs. Next Door could host church. She is the saint of little sandwiches, mending cuffs and gentle scolding. She matches her lawn ornaments. She walks like she is figure-skating. She carries a first-aid kit. She is always calling out the time. Bath time. Suppertime. Homework time. She is the cuckoo bird of mothers, something between a wind-up doll and a wax museum. Once, my sister, Immaculata, and I heard Mrs. Next Door tell the twins to stay away from us because we were macabre. The twins didn't understand *macabre*.

Mr. Next Door was a professional football player. Now he is just another formerly muscular man with a briefcase and a hatchback. Sometimes he looks at us lingeringly in the driveway. He smells of photocopier and he never tells jokes the way most men do. He just heads for their front door, withering into the shape of a question mark as he draws near.

One of the twins neighs while the other uses her skipping rope as a whip — just grazing her sister, who, below on all fours, does not dare look up for fear of blindness or disfigurement. 'Faster,' the one with the whip commands, 'faster, you filthy mare.' Too exuberant, she trips herself. She holds her scraped palms open as though she had been carrying something — a trophy, an infant, a glass slipper — and now it is gone. The horse sister neighs plaintively and strokes her injured sister with her double head. They look at me and together they sputter, 'You're bad luck, Eugenia.' I see them tangled in the underbrush of a lake, tangled in each other, drowning frantic and then perfectly, smoothly together.

'Snack time. Now,' Mrs. Next Door commands.

I do not want to leave my post, so I pretend to be looking at the teenage flowers poking their new oval heads out of the earth, and I pee. I pee in our garden, scant and brittle and doomed, in naked daylight.

All said, I am easily found. Find me. This is what my body yowls, even if I am all orderliness and composure. I am a spectacular quiet. A morgue after hours, empty corridors and, somewhere, a knocking from within.

The postman walks by. No mail. Still, he stops. 'Good day, little lady.' I know by his extra glee that he has no wife, no girl-friend, and that some nights he eats out of a can. 'Waiting for the tooth fairy?' 'No,' I say, flicking my front tooth back and forth, the dangler on a nerve string. 'The tooth fairy does not exist.' 'I disagree,' says the postman, enthusiastic, a man in a theme park. As he is about to launch into a fake fable, I cut him off, 'See you anon,' and I look beside him to make sure I am not missing my cue, a car door swanned open, a hard wink. I need to get him past me, past my line of vision. I want it unobstructed. I want everything unobstructed. 'Move along.'

The postman is gone. It smells like bachelor apartment.

I am synesthetic. When I smell, I see. I was diagnosed with synesthesia when Mink's perfume made me bite my tongue until it bled and scarred. A gully. She moved to smooth my bird's-nest hair, her skeleton wrist passing my face, her nails filed into darts, and with it, I saw bayonets slashing through the bodies of serpents.

I try to explain this, with my swollen tongue, to the doctor. His scalp is a freshly seeded lawn. His eyes, the colour of turpentine. He pats me down like dough. I stutter. I am all vowels. 'I ell er efum an ... aw ... erents ... an ayo.' I cannot find words or answers. This always happens when I am beside Mink. Like I have just arrived in this body and I am still trying to figure out how it works. Not the way I am with you; with you, I am *a dare-devil, an aerialist, a miracle*. Your words, not mine.

The doctor explains that synesthesia is thought of as a cross-wiring in the brain, a leftover from the early mammals. 'It often comes in the form of letters and numbers having specific colours.' As he speaks, his forehead winks white. He is an egg about to hatch. He is full of spiders. 'For instance, the letter F will come across as a sharp yellow; in turn, so will the words *finger, fog, faith.*' 'F,' says Mink. Mink is flushed and gleaming. Mink is turning into dessert. Mink and the doctor laugh the way adults laugh when they can't have sex. This haha is my hand between your legs and this other haha is my hand moving over your breast, a matador on a motorcycle, vroom, vroom. The doctor leads Mink behind the examination curtain for what Mink calls grown-up talk. There is an exchange I can't quite make out that involves the words *cheeks, lamb* and *parking lot* and then there is what sounds like a scuffle. They re-emerge from behind the curtain. Mink is unaltered the way she is always unaltered: flood, famine, mushroom cloud, everything would still be tickety-boo for Mink. Adjusting himself, up, down, the doctor goes on, panel-professional now: 'Synesthesia has a strong genetic component,' he says, all business, all comportment.

You see with sound.

'And is more common in the premature,' he concludes, subdued zing.

Me, by three months. A worm.

I trip on the way out of his office and split my lip.

'Eugenia,' Mink says as if I'm a stubborn stain, and apologizes to the receptionist, thick and square under two sweaters, both buttoned to the neck, nose chapped to a cardinal red. 'She's an incurable drunk,' and Mink laughs her throaty laugh. The receptionist hands me a tissue from her sleeve, 'There, dear, you're bleeding.'

Later, you tell me that if I were to surprise you on a busy city street, you would, upon seeing me, hear an entire symphony.

We live in Parkdale, a village in the west end of the city of Toronto, made up of Victorian mansions that used to border the lake. Women with parasols and bathing suits down to their calves, women with consumption, walked the beach, Sunnyside Beach. Now the highway sits on top of us, a beleaguered crown, turning Parkdale into a tired beauty queen. Feathers in her hair. Crinolines in a knot. She is grand. She is slumped. She is a rooming house with clapboard siding, transoms, cornices and turrets. Her voice is parched and playful. She is all invitation. She will take you in when nobody else will. The sun: her chandelier, her tarnished medal for bravery.

A shirtless man steers a shopping cart filled with scrap metal and stereo equipment. He wears a sleeping bag for a scarf. Inside our house, Mink will be plugging her ears, fingers forming an arrow, *What a racket*. The man's right eye is purple and swollen shut, the wet hump of an urchin. In Parkdale, he is not an unusual sight. It is the smooth faces that people stare at, the smooth faces that stand out. Everyone else appears shipwrecked. Everyone else appears collapsed with scurvy. Teeth falling out. Bones splintering into matchsticks. Eyes streaming with blood.

Morning turns into afternoon, the sun slinking slowly west, all sprawl and repose, and taking with it the freshness of the day. Immaculata places a sandwich beside me. Her long wrist, the lace cuff of her dress too short, a mess of blue veins. She has a stricken look, a sixteenth-century face the colour of porcelain. 'Sustenance,' she says in her nurse purr. She pads away. I look at the sandwich. It is isolation on a plate. The crusts have been cut. I open it. Liverwurst. No garnish. No condiment. This is Immaculata.

My older sister, the proletarian restaurant. She is all task completion. There is no waste. No frivolity. There is no humming
under the breath.

Suddenly she is beside me again, the human postscript, panting liver into my ear, 'When I couldn't find him this morning
to give him his coffee I thought he might have spontaneously
combusted because that would be just like Sheb and then I saw
the kippers and then I thought *strange* and then I realized that
he had left and my guess is that he is not coming back and that
this is it for a father no more father Euge no more father no more
Sheb.' She is so efficient there is no punctuation.

'Wrong,' I say too late. 'Wrong,' and I practice standing on
an acorn without splitting it. I do it. A perfect shot to the air.
Pow pow. Maybe you are watching. Please, be watching.

You tell me that an acute sense of smell can lead to impeccable
balance. You tell me that this is true of the Asian elephant, and
true of me. I set out to prove you right. And while I do, I imagine you, braided wire around your wrists, your waist, your ankles,
being slowly pulled up to standing by me, your small army.

Riding on your bicycle to Our Spot, *secret*, every night for this
past year, to dangle our lines in the lake and catch nothing, rain,
sleet, the last of the snow and ice melting into a dirty cross-section
of bone, a blown-out honeycomb around us, I say *Stop* whenever
I see the possibility for daring. You do. At first, in alleyways and
playgrounds, I balance forgotten balls on my forehead and then
catch them with the back of my neck. You clap. And then I
perform this same small motion with the slopes of a stranger's
roof falling north and south below me. You clap more – now

five people instead of one. *Stop.* You break into an abandoned factory (fist through window, *fuck*, scar), and with a ta-da of your arm, you say, 'Madame,' and there I use light switches as toeholds. I walk the heating ducts above the sewing machines, crawling with spiders and rust. I do handstands on the seamstresses' chairs. And then I do handstands on the seamstresses' chairs tipped onto two legs. In that sprawling emptied room, clapping, you are a crowd. Clapping, the factory is full and busy.

When I return to you, you bow, believing the daring was your own and you are invincible again; and I take your wrists, and I hold them where the braided wire would have been, the braided wire that pulled you up.

One week before you leave, you take me to the library. You breathe as though you have just been bullfighting. You have something to show me. You pull down a heavy book, the whole row with it, thud, thud, thud, not even noticing the bluster, and there in the stacks you say his name. *Finbar,* you say it in a whisper, *Finbar.* *Finbar* is a spell. *Finbar* is something you do not wish to disturb. You leaf through the book reverently, a family album. With it in your hands, you are no longer an orphan. You are the son of something. Something brave. Again and again, that week, we go back to the library. We go back to the same book.

> *I. I. Finbar Me the Three,*
> *Handsome Funambulist and Colossal Menagerie:*
> *An Unofficial Autobiography*

Again and again, the librarian tells us stiffly that we cannot take the book home. Even when you empty your pockets and offer her tobacco, spare change, a comb. Even when you plead with her, on our last day together, that Finbar is your father – the father who left you, twenty minutes old, in the maternity ward of a Kapuskasing hospital the night of the fiercest snowstorm the town had ever seen.

'Your father?'

'Yes, Eugenia. My father.' You stun even yourself with the announcement. And when it is made, it is like someone new has slipped into our room. With the exception of my birth, this is your quietest moment. Not used to it, I break it.

'But you have never mentioned him before.'

'It just came to my attention.'

'How?'

'You.'

And, in the hush of the library, you mime doing a handstand.

Finbar is a tightrope walker. The high wire. He ruled it flamboyant and firm. You show me photographs of him again and again, commenting on your likeness – though Finbar has what Mink would call *a face only a mother could love*. To me, he looks battered. Swollen in burls and hard waves like his bones are punching him out from the inside. They shoot through him, thoroughbreds in a gallop – his face, hooves in motion. I imagine running my hand over it. I imagine it shifting under my touch.

With your palette knife, you carefully cut the photographs from the book. When we are banned for life from the library, you tell the librarian, 'You have a neck like a stem, which, if I was intent on destroying flowers, I would snap.' And then you hold the cut pages up to your face, a mask, and you say, 'Boo,' and then you laugh, and then you say, 'Boo hoo hoo.' The librarian, shaking, frostbitten, says, 'Beat it, buster,' and you repeat, 'Buster,' and then we do beat it, with the push of a broad man in a blue uniform, cut pages falling from the book like bulky snowflakes, photographs of Finbar stuffed in your pockets.

When we get home, we close the door to your studio and we iron the crumpled pages flat with our hands, the tightrope a straight line again. Here is Finbar in nothing but dark tights. Swarthy, a handsome musculature, he pushes a baby tiger in a wheelbarrow on a wire the width of your thumb across Niagara Falls. The baby tiger and Finbar appear to be roaring at each other. And grinning. They appear to be in love. They are 160 feet above the gorge. Water churns below them: a death soup. Here is Finbar between two skyscrapers, cooking breakfast on a small stove, the classic: eggs over, bacon crispy, a potato onion hash, strong coffee. I imagine him lifting the coffee to his mouth, staining it. The wind gathers between the buildings. He salutes an airplane overhead. Here he is again, with a woman sitting straight-spined on a chair on his shoulders, flanking Florence, spires crooked behind them. She is tall, remarkably tall. Like you, she is instantly someone you want to know, someone you want to be shuttered in with. She waves to the crowd gathered below. Contrapuntal. They are dead quiet. A frieze. She flutters. Her dress is bandages and they are coming undone.

You tell me, 'The woman on the chair fell to her death seconds after that photograph was taken. Some drunk shook the wire.' And then you punch the wall of your studio, your fist immediately gloved in blood like you just birthed a calf. The blood is thick and it sticks to everything you touch. Making my cheek, my neck, my hair, me, red as you tell me, 'Some drunk shook the wire. Some drunk shook the wire.' Two scars form on your knuckles. Of the seventy-two scars on your body, there are only four that I was there for. This moment accounts for half. I wrap a towel around your hand and I kiss your knuckles through the reddened towel, and with my new, worried mouth I pretend I am a queen in wartime. You do too. And then you lean in, your moustache now balsam-waxed in the style of his, straight across your face, a right angle in a world without right angles, Finbar's words, not your own, 'The trick is to have a stunt that no one else can perform.' I see the words in the space between us. The lettering is gold and ornate.

'Did Finbar fall too?'

'He tried.'

Sometimes a slow dance, tonight a toppling – the sun sets decisively and night sweeps in, all dark majesty and menace. A Cheshire grin. The air: teeth. I eat the liverwurst sandwich. It is wood chips. It is ashes. I can hear the vacuum cleaner inside. It is the sound of accusation. Mink is cleaning. We have not spoken yet. There is no need. I will be gone soon and with my absence there will be one less thing for her to worry about. She will have to wait a few weeks, but then she can turn my bedroom into an exercise studio.

Across the street and five doors down, Meatball Marta draws her curtains closed. Of all the neighbourhood women, she is my favourite, the one whose affections I court. Her face is that of a film starlet reclining on a divan. Skin like butcher paper, lithe as an electric eel, she has a Polish accent even though she has lived here since she was a girl. When she speaks on the telephone to her relatives in Warsaw, it sounds like *cream eternity cream eternity cream*. She could have state secrets and a fan made of peacock feathers. She could have a young lover in riding pants. On her bed is a buffalo hide, a lantern shaped like a phoenix above it. Her apartment is full of candelabras. They are bronze and ornate, borrowed from Renaissance paintings. Mink calls her *the spinster in loungewear*. Marta is always dyeing her hair and apologizing to me for being moody. She collects old books. The Everyman's Library. Her apartment is sinking from the weight of them. They are stacked in her attic. She says, 'I am unemployed. I am existentialist. I have no reason to leave the house.' I go there to look at the engravings in the books and to admire the adventurers, tall at the helms of ships, heading into the great unknown. Surely that's still on someone's map, somewhere: THE GREAT UNKNOWN.

Now her lights flicker yellow, like gnomes live there and they are bustling beside a great hearth, like her hovel is the one you find when you are lost in the forest and need a heel of bread. For a moment, I want to go there and have her pat my head and speak to me in her hard syllables, bricks of gold. I want her to calm me. But I don't dare. I could miss you.

I see what you are thinking. Why you didn't come earlier. It is all clear. As the outlaw says, cocksure, swayback, wet toothpick in the teeth, I must be under the cover of darkness to be wrapped in a horse blanket and stolen away. *Pow pow.* Now is the time. I know all about night, its roominess. I watched the movies with you, our fingers tangling in the popcorn. You would roar alongside the lion and then the movie would start and you would sink to a squat and fall still as a disciple. That black-and-white stutter broadcast on a sheet in your studio: cowboys liver-spotted with dirt loping through teepees; mistresses in nightgowns, purse-sized rifle clutched in hand, boss-lover's blood seeping into the carpet below; a spy on his elbows inchworming under a French window. You would cry for a thing downed, for a thing won. You could not distinguish their world from ours. I could. But I would pretend the delusion. 'Huzzah,' you would say, 'huzzah.' Cigarette stem ghosting the air. 'Huzzah,' I would answer, like a good catch, 'huzzah.'

The last time I visit Marta, one week ago, she pats my head as she always does. She wears an oval locket around her neck. It is new. She will not let me see who is in it. Her hair is Chicago

Night Life Black and matted and she has not dressed even though it is evening. Her cheeks are flushed like she has been tilling a field of stone or weaving wool to make garments for hundreds of children. She is full of children. They are quiet hills growing inside of her. She smells like she is fermenting. When I ask her if she has a fever, she says, 'No, I am sanguine.' When I ask her if she is pregnant, she says nothing and pulls a book down for me, the shelf teetering as if it is a beginner stilt walker.

The book is about a girl three oceans away who invents a language for a rope. The girl transmits a series of desires and commands to her rope and, to her astonishment, it rises an inch off the ground, and then a foot, until it coils up and lassoes itself through the air, coming back to her feet, and it dances for her and then it dances with her and then she thinks she hears it chuckle.

The girl feels a closeness with the rope that far surpasses anything she has ever felt with human beings, even her grandmother, whose kindness is never cumbersome. This closeness, like an undertow, makes her go toward the rope and away from everything else. She repeats these conversations with the rope a thousand times a day. Always away from her home and her school so that she will not be mocked or called mad. Always in the same untravelled clearing in the woods, between the jackfruit and the betel nut, bamboo creepers, the jamun and the mango. Until she does not have to have any other conversations. One day, she looks around as everyone eats their meals and laughs and wears certain shoes and ties their hair the same way and she wonders, missing her rope: *When did I become so different from everybody else?*

'I know,' I tell the girl in the book. 'I know,' I tell Marta.

The girl leaves for the forest.

On the day that they are about to lock her up, the mad girl in the woods, her village is wiped out by a flood. But she is not, because she talks to her rope and it rises while she stands on it, lifting her to safety. She hovers above her village and watches its superstitions be washed and wrung clean. Before they are drowned, the villagers have a final glimpse of her. They think she is an apparition floating above them. But they are wrong. Things like this, a girl on a rope in the air, are not sudden or fake or heavenly. They are a slow coming. They are an accumulation of events. Much like the flood. It seems quick. Barrelling across the earth. But it is not. It has been plodding. It has been brooding. Yes, the water was loosened – but it had been groaning all the while.

{ POSTCARD FROM OUTER SPACE }

my darlin',

there is no blue here.
memorize blue.

your grand disappointment,
your only scar,
s.

Am I missing my code? Are the stars blinking a message? Are those car lights for me? Did they not dim and brighten? Was that a tapping on the roof? Footsteps on the path? A whistle? I know that if I see the sun strain itself against the sky, I will die. Please do not let this happen. Please do not let day come.

We did swear. Our thumbs cut and pressed together, blood as our witness, we swore. *Forever.* We both have scars to show for it. I look at mine now. Ephemeral as a smudge.

What if you promised yourself to others? What if you have a hundred daughters? Scattered, all of us waiting in our corduroy dresses on our front stoops, all of us with our indented thumbs. All of us, the useless boom.

I lean into myself, hugging my knees to my chest – a pull there, which, like the beginnings of illness, I want to ignore. And then I feel the pain in my jaw that comes when I won't let myself cry. It is akin to something being sprained out of inactivity. I have got to *pull it together*, as Mink would say, *pull it together*. I am nothing but frayed cords twitching sparks at their ends. And being broken is dangerous.

Immaculata drops a shawl onto my shoulders, a bag of rice from a float plane. 'Warmth,' she says to me and moves soundlessly back toward the house. And then she returns. 'It's so clean inside we could sell the house for a mint for a pretty penny Mink says come in for a rest I hate to think of you asleep in the out of doors the pervs you know it's late you know and most people die at four in the morning true and it's almost that time.' She is gone. And then, postscript, 'Mink has the toothbrush out.'

Mink has the toothbrush out to scrub away every detail of what life was before this day – until she can no longer lift her head if she has to. Your stubble in the sink will be flushed into the sewers.

Kill the evidence and you kill the life that was. This is Mink's economy. Her mathematics for living. She will reassemble herself. She will do it out of a physical compulsion that she does not understand. Mink is the only person on earth who is haunted by nothing. Of all of us, she is the only one who is truly invincible.

I see you. Coming toward me. The gait. Unmistakable. Gallant bird in an oil spill. Shimmering like celluloid. Silver. I stand to meet you. One quick look back at the house. And then back to you and you are gone. In your place, the sun. The sun and all its wretchedness snakes itself across the sky.

You are not coming for me because you are dead.

Only, you are not dead.

You are not dead because you fried the kippers, left the note, drew the tumescent monk, plucked the apple tree bare and took your bicycle. All this since you tucked me in some thirty hours ago.

Two policemen arrive this morning to find me, asleep on the front lawn, my underwear showing, my eyes the underbellies of spaceships, swollen and transiting. The shawl must have been stolen. I wake to them standing, stock-still as targets. Their boots are aggressively shined. They smell of swimming pool.

'Is your mother home?'

They are so tired, these men. They are so tired of asking people questions. I think of deranged pigs trying to eat their own ears. Is this what they do at the end of their day when they sit in their cruiser staring at a river, do they shift in their seats and try to eat their ears, so unfilled with answers?

One of them wears a turban. 'Will you please take off your turban and let me swing from your hair?' I'm not good at abbreviating the truth. *Pure, so pure,* you would have said. Mink would have snap-whispered, *What, were you brought up in a barn?* Loud enough for them to hear, reproach, reproach. And then she would have subtly winked apology at them.

'No,' the Turban startles. His partner, mime-white with a weak chin, repeats, 'No.' His voice does not match his face. It is much stronger. He is in a choir. He goes on, 'What are you doing out here, waiting for the tooth fairy?' It is a particular school of men, this tooth-fairy school. Not the one I am used to. They don't collect birth announcements. They don't bellow soft-rock anthems from the tops of telephone poles. They don't bite the cheeks of passersby — gently — and then hurdle fences, crawl beneath bushes and never miss a pond. *Skinny-dipping only!* Pinstripe suit hanging nearby.

These men don't walk bridges as viewfinders, imagining their bodies dismembered by the pavement below until, wrung out, they retreat into their bedrooms to finger the dark, to fall into their mattresses, the feathers and cotton coagulating in parts, cutting into them, *cut me, this bitter rind, taking root.* They don't suffer as you suffered. Because you are *pure, so pure.*

I see you in the Rosedale ravine, blinkless and shivering, your antelope frame folded against the trunk of a rotting red oak. You are the last of your kind. I have to find you. A novice crouched over a colony of mushrooms, you cannot separate the beauties from the poisons. Unsupervised, you will taste everything.

You take me camping once to Darlington, which also happens to be the site of a nuclear power station. You do not notice the spindly towers that straddle the landscape. Instead, the car a rocket, you steer it agog — back road after back road until the back roads end. It is the first and only time I have been outside of Toronto. You park the sedan in a ditch and scribble a sign on cardboard:

with my daughter

and then say to me, a man receiving a message from an eagle, 'This way.' You lead me through the unbeaten bush. You want to *live off the land*, so you bring nothing but a pack of matches. *How how.* You build a fire and we sit around it for two days in a tangle of trees and horseflies while you hitch cigarette to story to cigarette to story. You do not notice the groan of our empty stomachs, steamers turning back to shore. You are on a streak, your mouth wheeling unstoppable. On the third morning, upon my coaxing, we tear down camp, walk ten minutes to the sedan, slumped brown in the ditch. One of the windows has been smashed in by a tree branch. The sign is still there. We go to a nearby truck stop for coffee. The window glass is scattered sequins on the seat. The backs of our bodies shimmer dust and arrowheads. When we sit down, flecks of blood sprout beneath our pants. One of your eyes is clamped shut by bites. You steal the sugars and the creams, stuffing them into your suit pockets. *Just in case.* Just in case you cannot find what you thought you might.

When we get back to the city limits, scruff and abattoir, you hand me the pack of matches, carefully and with promise like it is a velvet box and in it are birthstone earrings. The cover says *REDBIRD. Strike anywhere matches.* I open it. There are two matches left. You profess, 'Best to go into the woods alone, Eugenius, then you'll find out for yourself.' It is the only gift you have ever given to me. I would watch you light matches off brick walls, the soles of your boots and, leg pulled up mid-march, the thigh of your pants. You would leave black skids everywhere, as though you were in prison and counting the days, the surfaces of the world your own primitive calendar.

I have to get you into a bath at the edge of everything, where it is tomb-quiet. I have to get a proper coat to you. And shoes. You are probably not wearing shoes. I see your long toes – your left big toe, yellow, the nail curdled and shrunken, because when you were growing, so astronomically, you were too shy to ask your adoptive mother, Plump Marie, for a new pair of boots – eventually you wore the black nail right off. I have to get you home.

I look up at the policemen, their aftershave faces. The Turban reaches down and offers his hand. My eyes fill fast, fast as a thing turned rabid, fast as a thing forgotten. The thud of this day, loud as a trampling. I finger the ground and feel the nudge of everything buried beneath me: infant bones, wooden spoons, the frames of houses lifting themselves to the surface and nosing the air, nosing me. I take it. The Turban's hand is much colder than yours would have been, but the grip is good. He has a monogrammed towel in his locker and wears plastic sandals in the shower. He has a gold medallion under his shirt in the shape of a cheetah. He never thought he would be a police officer. Sometimes, he and the Mime harmonize.

Mink answers the door. She turns on her beauty. It is persuasive as a milky thigh at a bus stop. The policemen will never forget her. When they drive by our street, when they hear the song 'Magic,' when they look at their wives rolling their stockings down into ankle doughnuts, they will think of Mink. Mink is a winner. Even when she is sleeping, she is winning.

Mink looks at me like I am a badly pitched tent. 'What has she done?'

'Nothing,' says the Mime defensively. He pops a piece of gum into his mouth.

'Are you trying to quit smoking?' I ask him.

'Yes. I am.'

'Because you're in a choir?'

'Yes. I am.'

'Sorry.' Mink ushers me in behind her and upstairs. Immaculata waits there for me. She drops her head on top of mine. I sit bolt upright, my feet tapping; we are a secret breathing in unison, a two-headed morning creature. Twenty feet of polar-bear-white shag carpet unspooled between us. Mink and her daughters. We are an entire tropic apart.

The Turban does the talking. The Mime just chews.

'Missus Monique Ledoux.' He says *Ledoux* like *LeDukes*, like she is all flying fists.

'That is me.'

'It would appear, ma'am, that your husband, Sheb Ledoux, has blown up a factory on the outskirts of the city. A shoulder-pad factory. He left a handwritten note behind for their security enforcement outfit to the effect that he is going to save the world and that he is — '

'An asshole,' says Mink.

'Correct. Have you seen him in the last twenty-four hours, ma'am?'

'No.'

'Heard from him?'

'No.'

'Do you expect to?'

She pauses. 'No.'

The Turban takes a breath, recalibrating. 'Is your husband violent?'

'Not violent enough.'

The Mime clears his throat. It is suddenly full of metal filings and wood shavings. He has walked into something hazardous with the possibility of collapse. He is sounding warning. The Turban goes on, undeterred.

'Were you his only – ?'

'Girls, to your rooms.'

We go. We open our doors. We close them behind us. We open them again. We return to the top of the stairs. We have missed it. Pinhole into the adult world gone.

'If you hear from him …'

The Turban passes his card to Mink.

'Thank you.' She studies and paws it. Still looking at it, she says, splicing her S's, 'He's sick.'

'How so?'

I can't see but I know that Mink is making a sign. My guess: a curt finger to the head.

'Suicidal?'

'Not yet anyway.'

Mink shifts in her stocking feet. And then there they go, the arches, tongues with destinations, they lift, all prance and flutter. Before she became the B-movie actress she is now, Mink was a professional dancer. Attuned to the interests of the times, she developed a coffee-house routine in which she lifted her leg above her head — slow as the hand on a clock — while swearing a blue streak in French. Her leg stopped at midnight. She became immensely popular. She signed her autograph on men's biceps and eyelids. She had a stalker. Her stage name was the Mouth. Her promise: 'I will make you blush.' This is when you first saw her. At Grossman's Tavern on Spadina Avenue. In a beaded evening gown, slits up the sides, matching elbow-length gloves, her left leg in the air contorted above her head, while outside, Chinatown, elderly couples with hospital masks doubled each other on their bicycles and coaxed slender eggplant from their front lawns. This, before the times changed. *Colline de bin de bobby pin, sac à patates, crème glacée molle, beurre d'arachide, au choco-lat, con, cul, couilles, chier, bite, nichons, putain, merde.* You saw her act so many times you had it memorized before you even crossed the room and introduced yourself. *Sheb Wooly Ledoux. Portraitist.*

Mink stands on the pads of her feet and then on her toes. Bedazzling, she comes to a sharpened point. She is a prospector and she is instantly six inches taller. She could drill a hole through the ground. The Mime and the Turban step back. Are there other tricks? Will she blow fire? Mink's feet are as gnarled as yours. Like a standard greeting, it is one of your only common-alities. Mink is surveying. The neighbours must have pulled open their curtains. Sensuous Marta and her fretting gnomes. Cruiser on our front lawn, blinking red, uniformed hulks in the doorway. We are the stage now. We are the players. Mink misses nothing. Especially an audience.

She topples to the floor. A melodrama of grief, she wails and sobs. But the performance has chinks in it, and it gets the better of her. It turns real. It turns sour. She cries, a thing snarled in a trap, nothing but the expanse of a deaf world around her, idiot hunter turned loose within it, knowing that she is alone in the woods, and that she will bleed to death, and that the only one who might have saved her is gone.

Immaculata slinks down three stairs so she can watch. I don't. I can't. I write a letter.

I have never seen Mink cry, except at sports on television. She cries at victory; finally, after this endless human slog, she recognizes one of her own. A champion. She does not cry at loss. When there was a fire around the corner from our house, the smell of tar and hair burning filled the air. The smell of old. Doilies, photo albums, a recliner and a basement full of hockey cards and comic books, all of it in an uproar of flame. In a trance, Mink excused herself from the dinner table and slid out the front door. When she came back hours later, she leaned her face in close to mine and said, 'She smoked in bed. The dunce. Everyone knows that one.' Mink was bored. Her face was hot from watching.

Now she has stopped working. Her mechanisms are sputtering and flailing. I do not want to see this in Mink. I do not want to see this mess. One thing in our life was supposed to be tidy, sure. One thing was supposed to never change.

The Mime has a coughing fit.

When the policemen start back to their cruiser, after Mink rights herself, a resurrection really, I run past her, a feral kitten, to the Turban. I hold a letter in my hand.

'Mail this for me. Promise.'

The Turban stonewalls.

'Promise,' I repeat myself.

He looks at the Mime. The Mime nods.

'Promise.'

'I don't have an address.'

I slip the letter, rolled into a scroll, into the Turban's hand. He looks at it; it is a baton and he did not realize he was running the relay. He won't even read it. His curiosity is that dead.

Walking away, they turn back one last time. Together they say, in different pitches, 'What if we don't find it?'

'What?'

'The address.'

'You will. You have to.'

The cruiser pulls away. One hand on the radio dial, the Mime looks at me. I wonder if he lives in a storage shed. I wonder if he wants me to live there with him and breed goldfish and play with a rescued, chewed-up doll on the sawdust floor. I wonder if he wants to change my name.

Walking back to our house, I see a glimmer in the grass. It could be the Mime's gum, the Turban's medallion, their bitten ears. It is my tooth, my last baby tooth, white, small, bloody at the root. It must have fallen out when I slept.

Mink waits for me in the doorway. From here, you could convince me that she is made out of marble, cut out from a block into this tiny, immovable shape. I hope she does not touch me. Or console me. I smile at her, wide, with my bar-brawl mouth, my incredible ugliness. These empty spaces, a baying. I am the mascot for what is missing. I am filthy. My eyes go dull. She lets me pass. I don't even know if she is breathing. She closes the heavy door behind us. I look up at her. Still, she is the colour of orchids.

Mink yanks the curtains closed. The show is over. The house takes on the quality of a cellar. Let there be root vegetables. Let there be murder. Let there be cards and cigars and whisky. Let there be pickling and ladies of the night missing pinkies and a dozen black cats idling in formation outside, their exhaust a potion to the air. Let our shoes be polished with beet juice. Let one of us be dead. Let it be me. A slit throat or, better, a bullet hole still smoking in the forehead, halos lifting themselves to the heavens. Let there be some kind of stringed instrument moaning in the corner played by a one-eyed sloth in a beige tuxedo. He taps his foot through the rotting floor. Potato bugs scurry for peace. We have been here for centuries. Deciding how to live. When, finally, the verdict comes down, intrusive as daylight.

'It is better to be widowed,' Mink says with the clarity of a snapped elastic, one burst blood vessel on her cheek. 'The funeral will be tomorrow afternoon. They're calling for rain.' When I protest, 'But he's not dead,' she says, 'He is not coming back, Eugenia. Waiting is for dunces.' She is all full stops – a telegram. Immaculata bows her head in shame or prayer, I cannot tell. Mink goes on, 'He could slip in the shower. Choke in his sleep. Fall down the stairs and break his neck. He could catch fire in any number of ways. He could have some crippling, surprise disease. He could be standing still and just die. A heart attack. A clot to the brain. To the lungs. Blood poisoning. A tropical flu. An arrow. A rabid bear. An elephant seal. Mouse droppings. Strangulation. A bone in the throat. He could be the victim of malice. A gang of thugs. He could drive into a telephone pole. He could drown in a culvert. He could be hit by a train. Gruesome has a kind of endless quality to it, girls. Pick.' She has foam at the corners of her mouth.

'Drowning it is rumoured to be peaceful and besides he could not swim,' says Immaculata with the fixity of a logician.

Even though you could not swim, you could splash. At first, it would seem you were attacking, pounding the water with your fists; it would come up in rapid shocks around you. But then, too quickly, you were being attacked by something flexible and all-knowing – something that, patrolling the shoreline, I could not quite see.

'Do you second?' Mink asks me. 'I need you to second, Junior Miss. I need you to second.' And then, the general flicking dander from her epaulettes, she says, 'Pull it together, Genie. Drowning it is. He drowned. In the lake. Fishing.' She glares in my direction.

Mink pushes her chair away from the table with a skid, turns on the radio and piles the clean dishes into the cupboards. When Mink does what she calls *women's work*, she is a robbery in reverse. Returning everything to its rightful place. The opposite of a thief, she is loud and careless. Daring the world to catch her, to find her out. Clattering, slamming, fighting the furniture, beating the carpet, huffing at the sinks, the shelves, the floors, Mink must keep track of all the misplaced pieces, for only she knows where they go. I wonder if this is what motherhood is: the noisy race, the impossible task of staging wholeness.

Mink starts to make dinner, wraps a tea towel around her waist instead of an apron, says, 'What the fuck am I doing,' throws the tea towel to the ground, tells me to stop my whimpering even though I am not making a sound, it is Immaculata imitating a mewling calf, which she does when she is afraid.

With that, Mink goes upstairs to her bedroom. There is not a step or a gesture out of place. She cannot help but be choreographed. Watching her round the stairwell, I wonder why it is that I am living with a perfect stranger. Roofs constellate and land on us like children who do not know their own strength. Family too.

Like a ghost baby, Immaculata follows Mink, her feet barely touching the ground.

The wind picks up. Like my mind, it is an itch. The creak and sway of the walls. The shift in the floors. The rattle of the windows. Without you in it, this house is unfamiliar. This house is not mine. The green fridge and matching stove, pot holders with beehives on them, a spider plant dangling behind the sink on a shelf with spices. Who lives here? And really, why should I?

Tell me, why did that woman around the corner burn along with her son's Scout uniform? Why did she stay in her bed swearing it all existed, that it was true — people used to live here and some of them loved each other — hand on her heart, cigarette in her mouth, the flames licking her knees, quick and feisty, carnival clowns? Why, when it would have been so easy for her to walk out the front door and through another one, the old love having been so well beaten out, a broom to a rug, that it does not even smoulder? Why is it that she stayed and you left, seamless as a good thief?

Or did you just need to lose yourself in the night? A deeper black than yours. A gangrene all its own. When you're sick, you love the sicker thing. Well, I can be sick too.

I sock myself. Right in the eye. Fist whistling through the sponginess of cartilage. It is the sound of a boy bouncing a ball once in an empty stadium. It is an excellent punch and the blood, obedient, my intimate, shoots itself to the surface and pools there. My eyes water, and then I am presented with pain. It wears a pressed suit. I welcome it. I shake its hand. It is a shape, something I can turn over and examine. The black eye is a relief. The boon to inflicting pain on yourself: you can predict its arrival. I look at my reflection. Slowly, it rises, the bruise, as though you left a jar of paint on my face to shimmer like the inside of your mouth. You would say, 'See, Eugenia, my darlin', everything's built for injury,' and then you would punch yourself too. 'We're the same.'

The wind again. Babble, babble, the entire world is telling its secrets at the same time. Mink returns. I can smell her. She has washed her face and put on fresh lipstick. Menthol and blubber. I sneeze. She stands behind me, hesitates, says, 'Hm,' and then she leans down and does exactly the wrong thing. She puts her hand in the centre of my back and runs it up to my neck, spiders losing their balance. She kisses me with a trace of her teeth on the spot where my spine meets my skull. *This is where the mother cats carry their kittens, Genie. Vets are trained to hold them here. It keeps the critters calm when they feel threatened.* Then she leaves. A cartoon tunnel. She is a dot shrinking in the distance. Not a perfect stranger after all.

I remember the cats in our yard picking up their litters by that loose skin, and how the kittens would immediately go limp. I throw up in the sink. And then I cry. I cry so much that I fog up the windows of the kitchen. By the time I lift my head and see what I have done — changed the ecology of the place into steam and salt — I want to show someone. I want to get Immaculata and I want to tell her: it is so weird how powerful we can be when we are sad. I want to tell you.

Instead, I stare at nothing. I am sitting for a portraitist and I am saying, *This is how we live, this is how we live.*

{ POSTCARD FROM OUTER SPACE }

my darlin',

one one thousand. two one thousand.

s

From the kitchen, night a black spill, I hear Mink in the living room doing her exercises. I know that she is wearing her turtleneck and her tights and that she is thinking to herself: *Why wear pants when you got gams like these?* She is so flexible she can kiss her own tailbone.

After Mink explained the scruff of the neck and its significance to a kitten, I asked her if she loved me.

'Of course I love you. I'm your mother.'

'But that's not real love. That's theoretical love. Like theoretically, I am deserving of your love because I am your daughter. But do you feel love for me?'

'How would you describe that?'

'There is no description. It just is. Everyone knows that one.'

That night she got out the toothbrush for the first time.

Last night was the third.

This is the letter I rolled into a scroll and placed in the cold but firm chlorine hand of the Turban while the Mime, tenor, said, 'Promise.' This is what should be in the mail by now, and maybe, just maybe, open on Finbar's kitchen table, his exploded face above it.

June 8, 1981

Dear I. I. Finbar Me the Three
Handsome Funambulist and Colossal Menagerie,

I will keep this brief as you are either very old or very dead. Though the unauthorized autobiography I have has been largely distressed by my father's palette knife, you are, by my calculations, eighty — if you are even living. I am nine. My name is Eugenia. My address is Number 101 Dunn Avenue in the City of Toronto, Mother Six Kidlet Two Robber Eight. I weigh eighty-five pounds. I am five feet tall. My mother is Mink. My sister, Immaculata. My father, Sheb Wooly Ledoux, portraitist. Last night, my father vanished. He left a note behind that did not include my name. I took this to be a sign that he was coming back for me. I think I was wrong. I think he might be on his way to you. This may take a while. He is not one for straight lines. In the meantime, if I had two words written on my eyelids and I was blinking, you would read: Rescue. Urgent. Rescue. Urgent. Rescue. Urgent. Sheb is a forthcoming sort. Forgive him this. And please forgive his lunatic ranting. Forgive him this at least until I get there too. If in doubt, give him an apple.

Whether this letter will even find you is another matter altogether, and one that I have little choice but to leave in the hands of two singing police officers.

Eugenia Ledoux

We sit in your studio and listen to Merilee Rush and the Turnabouts sing 'Angel of the Morning' for an entire day. Juice Newton just came out with a version, but this is the original and you insist on originals. You do not paint. A new canvas sits on your easel in the corner, a face waiting to be filled in. It is really just an eye. A left eye, floating. The only event of the day is the song. You say that you need to *understand the song!* We sit on the floor cross-legged like sages, reflecting each other − my hair, your hair, your eyes, my eyes, my face, your face. We listen, and every time it finishes you leap up, move the needle back again, scratch, scratch, to the beginning.

A hundred listens later, your beard that much thicker, as I am about to spell it out, you finally proclaim, 'I get it, Eugenius, I get it.'

'What?' I pounce back.

'She is saying goodbye. She is saying goodbye before she has to, while she still has the chance.'

The needle bumps over the blank space at the end of the record − a message being nervously tapped out. The unfinished face is your face. I look away from it to you. Tears skip into your eyes. And with that I see there is a whole layer of sadness to the world that I have not yet begun to uncover.

June 9, 1981. The backyard. Your funeral. Mother Mink Ledoux in black. Gloves and two girdles. Sister Immaculata Ledoux in white. Both: hair lined up and soldiered into braids. I am in your pinstripe suit, the one you left behind. Cut and sewed and shrunk. Cowboy boots too. Found glowing and snorting in a corner of the closet; I step into them, they fit.

You must have left barefoot. In your black suit. Your winter suit.

You have moved from the ravine now. South. Probably to a rooming house on Shuter Street. You are gathering your wits. Deciding on your next move. You have not slept since you left home. Your body is the hand of an elderly woman reaching for a teacup: shaking and determination. Piss-stained corridors, musty lighting of an old submarine, the rooming house has the quality of a thing that is sinking. It is full of coughing and lesions. Hair skidded across balding heads and overcoats, always overcoats, winter or no, usually with egg stains, hard, on the lapels. The lucky ones have a bottle in their breast pocket, hot as an extra heart. The others are draped on chairs staring at the communal television. It blinks its picture clean. In their rooms, the men's socks soak in sinks like dead fish. There is no one to call. They are all of the love letters the world meant to write but didn't. They have not been touched in years.

Until you. You shake their hands. You pat their backs. You pull their blankets up around them. You cut their hair. You call them *Captain* and *Colonel* and *Corner Office*. You tell them stories and your stories become the only flicker in their world, bright as a flare, bright as a son. By the time you leave, without a word, they would have called you their own.

Immaculata is playing her autoharp; she has plugged it into the living room speaker system with extension cords. There is a jumble of cables in the grass, the head of Medusa. I hope that it does not rain. Immaculata hopes that it does.

The sky is wet newspapers. Beneath it, brimming, the women of the neighbourhood appear. Whenever you rode by them, a centaur on your bicycle, they shouted, 'You're so skinny, Sheb! Come to my house! I'll feed you proper!' while waving a handful of mail, their wrists all bracelets, a clatter to the air, Cleopatras with heating bills. Because you interpret everything as an invitation, you would go to her house and she would fuss over you like you had been returned from war, her mouth painted coral, eyes batting like grasshoppers. You would sit in her kitchen and you would tell her stories of heroics. Always your own.

It never seemed like gloating, only that every second with you would give her good luck. And she would tremble on cue and shake her head incredulous. You would abbreviate her name and then you would tell her it was the best meal you had ever had and then you would kiss her cheeks three times, never more, and come home full. She would fall asleep feeling like a child, all of her lumps and aches vanished, her husband's hairy back a sleeping ogre beside her.

I know the women by their laps and arms. They put me on their knees and lean over me, bodies like hair domes, burning and breathy. They want to win my affections. They know that I am the password to you. They never say my name, they sing it, *EuGEniA*. On this day, they are all turned out. Beside Mink, they are the beauty contestants who lost.

Skinny Selene Valadan and her hound-dog eyes. She smells of laundry soap. She never sleeps, just climbs a mountain of dirty clothes, her children scrambling for cover within it. And here is Clotilda from next door, a chess piece with her long grey braid, its brittle end. She talks about deadbeats while her roommate, Yufeng, in matching printed smock, says, 'Oh brother.' They carry grocery bags filled with stale bread for the pigeons and peanuts for the squirrels. Clotilda has a son who never speaks. Mink calls him *Lee Mute*. He fixes cars outside their house, spray-paints them silver, glues naked lady stickers on them and never meets my eyes. Once, I hear him sing through the wall. In tune. With a drum machine. Here is Tuberculosis Flo in her sneakers, white hair pulled back with a hair band, track suit bulky like there is a tutu stuffed under it. Lungs full of slugs and marbles, she is always coughing into the crook of her arm. She says, emphatic, 'Don't you worry, it's not contagious.' She has to repaint her walls once a year, the corners of her ceilings twice, so yellow are they with smoke.

Elsie isn't here. She is war-bride old, eleven-children old, one-room-schoolhouse old. When she sees an airplane overhead, she says, 'Who knew.' She has a silver pin from the government that she wears on her quilted housecoat for being one hundred. Her age makes me think of centipedes — their slim bodies, so vulnerable, darting underfoot. She credits her longevity to eating herring from the can. Immaculata visits her once a week and reads to her. Recipes from back issues of women's magazines. This is what Elsie enjoys more than anything, knowing how to braise a pot roast and score a ham, even though her house emptied itself a long time ago. I think Immaculata goes there in the hopes that she might find her dead. That would make three. The heart attack at the Roti Lady Restaurant. And the hobo who would not answer, 'Would you like some it's juice it's grape it's good you look thirsty are you thirsty?'

Leopold of the Onions is also missing. He lives up the street. He is allergic to the sun, part of a marching band on weekends and wears a medical bracelet. He is eighteen, though he is small and hairless and still prone to the fits of a child. He would have begged his mother to let him attend your funeral. He would have gotten the hiccups and given himself a nosebleed, and he would have been forbidden.

Marta opens the gate to the backyard. When I look at her, I am looking through a smoky glass. Her hair is dyed Tiger Tail Orange. She wears a black pantsuit with a thick patent-leather belt. She gives me a jar of meatballs. She does not pat my head the way she usually does, her arms and hands are so weighted with lead. She is full of anchors.

Upon Marta's entrance, Mink holds both of our hands so hard that I will have welts. Skin: bleach and sunburn. Immaculata will not. She does not mark the way I do. Her scars require more resolve. She belongs to pain. Pain is her pedigree, her club. Her measuring stick for being alive. 'Painfully alive,' she will say to me in a rasp-whisper when she tells me about women skinned slowly by oyster shells and horses made to run deserts with toenails too long. I never forget anything. The women's skin in ribbons. The horses' weepy lurch. To fall asleep, Immaculata reads the recipes of the medievalists. I don't read this stuff myself, but I can hear her through the wall. She acts it out in her room, a fencer skittering, all exclamation points.

Just as we are about to begin, one-hundred-year-old Elsie arrives. She smells of mildew and lilacs. She wears a silk turban accented with a glittering brooch. She hands Mink a stack of cardboard perfume samples torn from magazines, a can of herring for me, and for Immaculata her silver pin from the government.

Immaculata puts down the harp. The rain starts.

My eyes are round wet blisters, drowned featherless birds. The smell of your kippers fried, and then burning, spikes the air lime-green, tarnished silver. It lingers, your attempt at breakfast, two days later. The weather patterns: nausea. My boot heels dig down into the grass, leaving sinkholes for the rain.

The twins next door practice a dance routine. They are the colour of pinch. They cartwheel in matching leopard-skin leotards and headbands. Land. Bound up in unison, all nipples. Land. Nostrils flared, square-shaped contestant smiles across their faces imagining a panel of judges. They sing under their ragged breath, the call-and-answer of bad mating:

'Well, you're a real tough cookie with the long history.'
'Of breaking little hearts, like the one in me.'
'That's okay, let's see how you do it.'
'Put up your dukes, let's get down to it!'
One contorts her hips. One doesn't.
'Hit me with your best shot!'
The one who doesn't slaps the one who does.

Finally, Mink clears her throat and says, 'He left the toilet seat up. Took the change off our dresser. A pack of matches. The apples. His bicycle.' She pauses. 'And Eugenia's baby hair.'

A faint crack across Immaculata's face. The apple tree, denuded, its branches moving, hands desperately trying to cover up.

And then, 'I loved him.'

Before we were born, Mink played every great part. Black-and-white photographs of her line the hallway between our bedrooms. She is the drowning virgin, the duplicitous queen, the misunderstood saint, her face tilted up, a conductor for the light. Like Immaculata, bereavement suits her. Mascara spills down her face. Otherwise a study in placidity, it is powdered a stark white. Thick drops of black Jackson-Pollock her skin. Museum face. Her tragedy is neat. Her tragedy is art.

Again, she says, 'I loved him.' This time to herself. She sounds surprised.

I knew this. I knew she loved you because it was impossible not to. But still, these are the words that tip me over. I swallow hard and there it is, that sprain in my jaw.

Mink lifts her head, a woman with a sword in her side who refuses to die. Her morbid cry. Pale and victorious. Liberty leading the people. 'His lips were like two steaks in the desert.'

There is no snot. No quiver. Mink is a widow with the posture of an electric chair.

I lean, crumpled, into her waistline, hoping that composure is contagious. Against the fine combed wool of her dress, her perfectly placed curves and bends, love shoots through me like the bombed fish flying. My heart presses up against my ribs, begging for release. I open my mouth, take in a hot slice of breath. I short-circuit. I faint.

I am unconscious for seven seconds. Immaculata times it. It is a rehearsal for death. Death is a blank. And then,

Snap. Snap. Snap.

I wake up to Immaculata's oval face, an antique dish, her hand fanning the air. I stand. Pain. She belongs here. I don't.

Mink concludes, her final breath, 'He is dead. Drowned. In the lake. Fishing.'

A tear falls from her purple eyes. It is plump, exquisite.

There should be a sandstorm. The sky should rain blood. We should be trampled by bulls.

The twins press their heaving bodies against the chain-link fence. Despite their interest in us, they cannot help but finish their song, as if it is a prayer they don't believe in but are too superstitious to leave hanging.

'Hit me with your best shot!'

'Why don't you hit me with your best shot!'

'Hit me with your best shot!'

'Fire away!'

It's over. The twins fall still, save for slow-motion gum-chewing. Then, cattle sensing a storm, even this stops. Their legs are goose-pimpled now — maroon sausages shot from their leotards. They stand thick, bellies rounded, necks buried under chins, faces painted Easter eggs. They shake and stare — horny puppies. Their teeth chatter a high-speed symphony. They send each other telepathic messages. I turn my eyes on them. Green, translucent, yours — they are the surface of a dead lake, life coiled and lost beneath.

Frightened, the twins spring away from the fence. They shriek through their plastic patio furniture, around their empty pool, the croquet set, the swings and the horseshoes. They stub and scrape themselves on every sharp edge. One will have stitches on her face, her pink cheek sliced open — War Paint Barbie. They slam their screen door shut behind them. Chimes echo in their cavities.

Peace at last.

Mink strokes my hair. It hurts. Then she looks at me, a chase scene. She is signalling that it is my turn to sing. I look up to the sky. It clears for a moment. A white bird flies by. And then there is a rainbow. Everyone thinks it is for us. That the earth has turned poetic because of death. But really, it is just shifting unknowingly, a great lazy beast crushing everything in its midst.

Immaculata picks up her autoharp. She gets small shocks as she accompanies me. I sing. I sing our song. It is an anthem. Remember our country. Come back to it. Come home.

> Just call me angel of the morning, angel,
> Just touch my cheek before you leave me, baby.
> Just call me angel of the morning, angel,
> Then slowly turn away from me.

Meatball Marta mouths the words.

I finish the song. Elsie dies for a second. Her eyes close, a horse sleeping at noon. Tuberculosis Flo applauds and then lights a cigarette inside her track jacket. Elsie's eyes open. The others join in the applause. The sound of confused animals running into walls. We are the grief brigade. Mink looks out to say that there has been enough clapping. The clapping stops. She lifts the lid off the Crock-Pot. She cues Immaculata and me. We reach into it in scoops. It is the ashes from our fireplace. We throw our hands out, fists blooming, our father and bits of junk mail, leaning, riding, floating up and eventually eaten by the wind. No one notices the adverts for drill bits.

Clotilda and Yufeng pray and then the formation of the neighbourhood women breaks. Talking to me in consolatory tones, they look to the ground and wring their hands as if they have all lost their wedding rings. They leave behind baked goods. Flo's smell of smoke. That night, we eat pound cake and spicy meatballs. Our clothes should be torn. Faces smattered in dirt. Our mouths should be open and empty like we have just seen our first public hanging. Instead, we gorge ourselves. Especially Mink. She has just come home from hunting.

While dragging her fork across the table, she says to me, 'You are the man of the house now, Genie.'

I sock myself in the other eye. The good eye. A thing ashamed, it swells shut. Mink and Immaculata don't even look up from their plates.

e,

i sleep with my chin in the air. you would call me
an aristocrat, offer me a bonbon, hiccup, slur
and then laugh your little laughs.
ha. ha. ha. back.

s

I grab your French cigarettes from the freezer.

Mink piques, 'And what are you doing, hm?'

'I'm the man of the house now.'

I run the bath, peel off your suit and leave your mud-thick boots standing inside the hem of your pants, like a firefighter, like you would do. I slide into the tub, skid, and I hear the voice of God. He is telling me to smoke. It is the first time I hear his voice. It is threatening. *Smoke!* He does make the thunder. *Smoke!* So I do. I light up.

Immaculata follows, her frond fingers unbuttoning her white dress. It drops to the floor, a flirtatious handkerchief. She lights a cigarette and sits across from me – bending her body, a pale fan folding. 'A preacher with a microphone in one hand and a baby in the other while sprinkling holy water on the baby's head he electrocuted himself whoa.' She smiles wanly. I don't. I cannot find the muscles in my face.

Immaculata should never go outside because her beauty makes her unsafe. It is a high note breaking the glass in your hand. Men spend their days wondering if she will draw her curtain aside. They memorize her dresses. They are all white. The men appreciate that. It's consistent. As if it's for them. A code. They imagine her in miniature dancing on their fingertips. They create a whole life with her in their heads. What she wants for breakfast. How she will nod at them with grace. How she will not mind their habits. How she will fetch them things and rub their necks. Her nightgowns, their ruffles. But when she walks by them they cannot move. They are just men with toothbrushes in their breast pockets sleeping in their cars in front of our house. They are just useless bits of glass that can never be made whole again.

In the bath, our sleek white bodies are stretched out into flags of surrender. I am hypnotized by this lagoon of soapy water. Between us, I blow circles of smoke in the damp air. I scorch my lungs until my dandelion head rises and pops off my spine. Rings hover above me. They are spaceships and ghosts and epitaphs. They are hints of an alternate universe.

Mink opens the door. The steam in the bathroom evaporates and leaves all of the surfaces in wet lines. Everything is the face of a broken woman. Mink is wearing her black silk robe with the Chinese dragon on the back. She has a white robe for the morning. Black is for night. She never switches them. The morning and the night dragons match. They are gold with formidable teeth. They have fangs, they breathe fire and they are sewn into a fight without repercussion. No one ever loses.

Mink paints her lips red. It is a red that she told me was a nightshade red. Nightshades kill. Hemlock is a nightshade. It killed Socrates. Everyone knows that one. When I first heard Mink say, 'I have to put on my face,' I was afraid that she had a trunk of faces and she would come downstairs as somebody else. This meant that if we were at the beautician's together and Mink went to the ladies' room and didn't come back, I wouldn't know which customer was really my mother. Anyone could have tried to convince me. So I used to watch her, my feet dangling over the counter, as she applied her concealer, her foundation, her eyeshadow, blush, mascara and lipstick to make sure that she stayed herself. And she did. Mink. Always leaning into the mirror, putting on her face. To me, a death mask. The rest of the world: possible mothers.

I lift my hands above my black eyes and wave them in the air. You told me that if I am ever stranded in the woods and an airplane circles overhead, wave with two hands. This means: HELP! Most people wave with only one hand. This means: A-OK. Then the pilot tips his wings and he disappears and you starve, found upon first thaw. A skeleton in a winter coat. One dumb hand in the air.

Immaculata waves back. With one hand. A-OK. Small, like I am behind the window of a dollhouse. Mink doesn't. She is busy. Perched on the toilet seat beside us, lighting cigarettes one off the other, she smokes in deep drags and exhales in all straight lines. It is geometric. I bet her organs are too. Her heart is an octagon, and she will be exhumed by a mathematician who will store it in a jar and bring it to bed with him where he will rub it and sing it ballads from the old country.

Mink's eyes are fastened on her own reflection. If she blinks, we too will vanish. First her husband, then her daughters, her face, her faucets. She is keeping us here. She is *pulling it together*.

We are less than one year apart, Immaculata and I. Six months and three days exactly. They call this Irish twins. Immaculata is born after seventeen hours of labour. You are frenzied, lapping the hospital corridor, lit bright as a fish shop, smoking and tugging at your clothes as though they are shrinking and soon you will be naked. You are not allowed into the birthing room, the nurses remind you. You offer them apples, interpretive dance, a nose kiss. They are tempted.

Mink, her face detonating, her body a yowling hell, curses the obstetrician at her feet. Ear pressed to the door, you join in. *Colline de bin de bobby pin, sac à patates, crème glacée molle, beurre d'arachide, au chocolat, con, cul, couilles, chier, bite, nichons, putain, merde.* Mink keens and, finally, feels her tenant leave the premises. And you, boxed by the sudden silence, burst into her room, a tornado.

The child is a fresh ballet. Her toes are long, her hands too. She is languid and ravishing as a mermaid. Her lashes are a perfectly curled inch of wet black. Her eyes are a most miraculous purple. She enters the world with one cry and has not cried since. Mink names her Immaculata.

Mink takes to motherhood instantly. She grows her garnet hair long and watches the muscles in her arms rise and tighten as she hoists her daughter about, slings her to her hip, lifts her up in the air and holds her to her breast for hours at a time, listening to the soft whale sounds she makes as she feeds. She is so thankful, her daughter. Mink takes her everywhere. Baby as decoration. Baby as corsage. It is the world of strangers that has Mink hooked. Bending and peering, they revere the baby. The whole world has leapt to its feet and is applauding Mink for what she has made. And for the first time, she is alone on the stage. All of the noise is for her and it is deafening. It makes her heart, that octagon, split into smaller units. But Immaculata will surely grow and learn to walk – eventually away – so Mink wants another one immediately.

I am born three months premature on the kitchen floor in less than twenty minutes. Mink later jokes that my birth is like a one-night stand. 'Quick and dirty. We didn't even make it to the bedroom.'

You move in strides, breathing along with Mink in exaggerated baritones. You see the crown of my head cropping up, a siren in the kitchen. You pull me free. You sever the umbilical cord with your palette knife and place me on Mink's chest. My mother: smooth as the skim of a frozen pond – one that, with its darkened centre, no one has dared to cross. Slick, white-blue, I have a full head of black hair standing on end. And one tooth. Surprise. Mink looks at me and I can hear the chatter in her brain. It is ticker tape: runt, whelp. I shriek. I am a tadpole, a thing birthed in the wild. I see a moose kicking away its young. She hands me to you. My father. I fit inside your palm. We lock eyes. I am quiet. So are you.

You refuse to call an ambulance. You refuse to leave the house. You refuse to go to the hospital. I am almost three pounds.

'She is the size of the world's smallest cat his name is Mister Peebles,' says Immaculata, already talking. Mink scrubs the floor with lye until it goes from red to pink to white, until she can no longer lift her head. It appears to her as the site of a massacre. Her own. And there don't seem to be any other witnesses.

Blown back into a corner of cupboards, the aftermath of an explosion, you hold me to you, your smallest finger in my mouth, a succour. You are a heat lamp. In your arms, I grow hesitantly. In slow and suspicious inches. To tonight. Five feet tall. Eighty-five pounds. And my heat lamp is gone.

Immaculata coughs, the bathwater splashing the edges of the tub. She coughs again. It is an imitation of the first cough. Without breaking her reflection, Mink claps Immaculata hard on the back. Immaculata's face turns to glee under a blanket. The smoke is suddenly spears in my throat. I stub my cigarette out in the marble soap dish. Tap tap. And now that we are in conversation, I say to God that I quit smoking and I welcome his wrath. I could use the attention. Go ahead. Drown me. I hold my breath. Cheeks puffed out, I slide under the water.

Floating there, in that waterlogged quiet, I remember the moment of my conception. My parents are under sheepskin in the afternoon, sun fissuring the blinds, turning everything to honey – even the dust helixes are made of sugar. My parents are good at sex. Aside from their feet, this is their other point of commonality. Their other standard greeting. They twine each other, Immaculata – their perfect halfway point, never a cry – is bundled between them, an elegant cocoon. They have not slept for three days, my parents, dreaming her and each other, slithering through blood and wishes, pooling themselves, and then me: a collision in sharp edges.

See, I cannot shake anything. I cannot shake anything because my brain is a weakling. Whip-skinny, it wants to fight everything and everything wants to fight. Drum roll.

This is my brain: a stranger on the streetcar with a runny nose playing the flute. Mink in her dish gloves throwing out a half-finished jar of mustard because it no longer looks neat in the fridge. How when we are camping, the stars are the confetti left on the floor of the legion hall. How when I tell you this, you say that I should write every book that is ever read. I wonder for a second if this could happen. And then I think that you are bad for me. And then I think that you can hear this thought so I stamp it out but it still burns. So I picture the van that was parked down our street for a year that had no seats in it. And that it could house a very small opera sung by the shortest man in Parkdale, Leopold of the Onions. Lettuce. Pyrotechnics. The hole in the end of my tights that lets my big toe poke out. How it used to be a recluse and now it is a showgirl, how it has stopped drawing cartoons and become one. Your last words to me. The sound of them in my ear. The feel of your mouth there, a storm rolling in. This is the worst fight my mind is in. It is a brute. It always lands its punches. They are square and straight-faced and they don't negotiate. I search out other smaller fights but I am down. The bell rings. A small man in a black bow tie declares: *It's a knockout.* And just when I start to get up and find my bearings, there they are again. Your last words to me. *Smack.*

Find me.

I wish for one blank moment, one flatline moment, but just when I think I am alone in my head, a parachutist with nothing but the wind, those words crop up. They are the ground rushing at me from below.

The bathwater is loud as an isolation tank now. It is lodged in my deaf embryo ears. I am zero gravity. I continue to hold my breath. What little is left rises to the surface in tiny bubbles.

Once you cried while we were listening to the radio. You pulled it to you like a friend who had gone out of his mind and wanted to cause himself harm. You shook it while it spoke. You tried to reason with it. *No. No.* A group of whales was stuck in a chain of northern lakes. There was only one hole in the ice for them to breathe through. The whales were taking turns breathing through the one hole. But they were running out of oxygen. Already, some of them were falling into the deep never to return. They were all going to die. A team of hunters and scientists was on its way to kill them. This is mercy, you told me.

I don't want my oxygen anymore. Take it.

Mink pulls me up by the hair like I was a kitten in a pillow-case and now she wants me for a pet. Immaculata examines our cabled shapes. 'What a polite thing to do,' she commends Mink. 'Death for life a clean trade I have learned something' She has unburied our family crest. 'Save people.'

I take in a deep breath. The air is a battle cry. Your French cigarettes. Bombs and redcoats in the distance. Shivering hands holding open maps. They were the kind of cigarettes you bought from your special man at your special store. You bought your coffee from another special man, greens from another and meat from another. The meat man. The greens man. The coffee man. The cigarettes man. They dot the city, these special men, and you were bonhomie to every one of them. You knew their wives' middle names and their parents' diseases. Together, you spoke in exaggerated gestures like you were doing a show for deaf children whose wondrous faces were pressed up against the window, the world an aquarium to them. You spoke in Greek and Yiddish and Polish. Yours was cobbled together, but your pronunciation was so perfect it was as though you had lived there and you really were brothers.

We would walk into their stores. The smell of oil paint and urethane coming off you, spiralling in the air in whips and sinews. A bullfight. I was tall as your belt buckle. I watched it shimmer telepathic. You would lift me up so that I could ring the bell. When I did, I could see into the back room. The special man would scuttle to a leather case, pull out a hand mirror, flatten his hair and eyebrows with his saliva, pop a mint into his mouth, lick his lips and undo his top button. Arms open, he would emerge victorious; he had just stepped off a plane and his stock was screaming his name. 'Monsieur Ledoux,' he would say, shaking your filthy hand – long and gangly and sure. He would shake it as if you were a tourist and his town were dying. 'Welcome.' He would yield to your every request. He would take you into his storeroom. He would unlatch the backs of refrigerated trucks. He would lift lids off boxes that had not been opened in years. He would dig up his mother if you thought she might be the freshest.

When we left, I would feel sad because these men now had to bide their time before you would return again and who knew when that would be. You weren't sad. Nothing would cling to you. You would already be inside the next moment. Time with you, in compressed portions. Time with you: all poems.

I open my eyes to Mink. My hair is still in her palm. It is a root system dug up. It shivers in the light. It wishes to be underground. Mink has broken her reflection. But it is not us falling away. It is her. She stares at us. Her lips quiver. Her face sinks. Smoke comes out of her nostrils in tailwinds. She is a dragon collapsing.

I walk out to the backyard, hair still wet, like I have greased it for a fight, my body too, slick in your shrunken suit and boots. Your stray cats climb out of the dark and into my arms. Their bodies beat warm in my hands, their hearts striving, bombs in their chests. Tails curl up into ties around my neck, bracelets around my wrists. They are a coat that flexes. I attach small bags to their backs filled with two feedings each of your bony fish and a small note that reads:

> *I have been abandoned.*
> *Please be kind.*

And then I toss them. Straight-legging their way through the air, onto the sidewalk in front of our house, they land in unison, bored cheerleaders. They look back at me with vague accusation, and then they walk away, a funeral procession up to King Street. I watch them shrink with the horizon. Another unrecorded moment of loss in the world. Another notch in the invisible gloom. The strays made strays again.

You told me that to hunt something, you have to become the thing you are hunting. I cut my hair in the style of yours, a slice across the front and a slice across the back. I bury it, making my bare hands black. The twins watch me. They are in their nightgowns, freshly bathed, their hair combed down flat against their foreheads. They glisten, open wounds. Their teeth: kindling. I let them watch me, knowing that I possess a higher magic, the hard worm of my grief. I am the widow. I am full of spells and incantations, languages they never knew existed. I have snuck up on them and won the race. Their sombre faces strain through the chain-link fence, legs overbandaged from their earlier collisions.

I walk toward them. The one with the gash across her cheek moves away. I hold up my hand, white-flagging. 'Sorry,' I whisper, my voice hoarse, a scrape to the air. I take in their faces: fruit growing hollow. The other one wants to touch me as though she paid admission. I won't let her. She pulls her hand back through the fence and says, caterpillar lips, 'It's okay.'

'Yeah. It's okay.'

'We know what a difficult time this must be.'

'Yeah.'

'Yeah.'

'We know suffering.'

'Yeah.'

'We are baking some stuff for you right now.'

'Cookies and casseroles.'

'Our personal favourites.'

'From a Betty Crocker cookbook for kids.'

'It's excellent.'

They hop.

'When we're ten, we can make pastry.'

'Yeah.'

'Pastry is tricky.'

'We'll bring the baked goods by.'

'Tomorrow.'

'If that's okay.'

'Yeah. If that's okay.'

'You could sell them if you're not hungry.'

'No. You couldn't.'

'Yeah.'

'Eugenia?'

'Yeah, Eugenia?'

'We want to make a pyramid.'

'We want to make a pyramid. Eugenia.'

'And a pyramid takes three.'

'Eugenia.'

'We want you to play with us.'

'You.'

'Play with us tomorrow.'

'Wanna?'

I can smell their breath. Toothpaste and vanilla. Premature death. Mrs. Next Door sees them and calls out, 'Bedtime. Now.' I watch them vanish past her. She forms the curtain to their world.

The lights of the twins' house are turned off so quickly. For them, the sky is choked with bombers.

Where is my sign? My bundle of clues? An arrow. A homing pigeon. 'It is I, Eugenia, your daughter beloved.' I mouth this up to the apple tree. Its licked branches against the night sky, the strokes of the first alphabet. I wave two hands in the air, *help*, but the world is unmoved. A mute witness.

The twins' house is a black eye now as they are pressed between their sheets and worried into sleep. Mr. Next Door comes out onto the back porch and lights a cigarette. He does not even pace while moths throw themselves at the porch light, suicides fast as fetal heartbeats. I listen to his inhalations and exhalations. They are the breath of a sleeping beast. I crouch to the ground.

Children lose their minds the way that adults do. Same as adults, we have various strategies to win our minds back. Immaculata told me about a girl who did equations in her head to fall asleep at night. The equations were very sophisticated. The numbers made her less distraught. And they kept the witches away. If you have a million birds flying in your head, it makes a difference if you can name them. All of that skittering. Name the birds. Only then can their calls be separated. Only then can their beaks be blunted.

You ride the shoulder of the highway, wheels spitting up gravel. A grimace on your face. Beard: hoarfrost. Cheeks more sunken, more hungry than usual, you're thin as a line drawing. You think to yourself, *I was supposed to be hero to something but I have forgotten what that was.* Me. You were supposed to be hero to me.

You did not write *eugenia* on the note because you could not. I would have tripped you up. I was your last bit of health. I would have kept you here. When you ride, you hear a sound in the brush travelling, running alongside you. Sometimes you stop to see if it is animal and sometimes you stop to see if it is human.

Tonight you build a fire in a farmer's field, and you burn, like diseased livestock, my photograph and my baby hair, and you fall asleep to the smell of me being licked away until I am black curls and ash. But you make the mistake of speaking to me when you are tired, a child who is lost on his way home, all of his landmarks inexplicably gone. You are not able to erase me from your mind. No matter how much your fists bleed from being scraped against rock, I am a noise there. A rattle. With the totems gone, the photograph, the hair, the thing you once wanted to remember and now try to forget is no longer fastened. It is freed and so it takes on a life of its own. I am freed. Framed by empty night, I take on a life of my own. The end of you. The beginning of me.

Marta stands in our yard in her black pantsuit with its cinched waist, her swollen face too rouged. I gasp when I see her. She came home from your funeral and, with an oven mitt on, loosened all the light bulbs in her apartment. It seemed to be the only thing she could do. She put on blush before leaving again. She wished to be civilized. She put it on in the dark.

Oven mitt still on, she hands me a rope, coiled into a perfect O, and says with the offering, guttural, 'A gift. Purely symbolic. Otherwise useless.' From the story. From the story about the girl who stood above the flood. I loop the rope around my shoulder. It sits heavy as if a ship hangs from its end.

'Thank you.' I look up at Marta, her desperate weariness. She has just been pulled to shore. So close to perishing, she cannot afford to be giving anything away. Too much has gone missing already. Habit, she touches her throat. Her locket is not there. She lets her hands fall. Arms still too tired to pat my head. 'You're welcome,' Marta says, walking away, a straight black seam completing the night.

{ POSTCARD FROM OUTER SPACE }

e,

there are astronauts lost in space. bolts,
gloves and tanks too. they float toward fires.
for days, for decades. sometimes, centuries.
just waiting to catch. everything, all of us just parts,
waiting to fall to the ground.

bring tobacco.
bring apples.
bring you.

sssss.

If Marta's rope were laid flat on the ground, and there were no apartment towers or highways to negotiate, it could, from our backyard, reach the lake. It is as long as Finbar's walk across the Niagara Gorge. As long as Finbar's walk between the skyscrapers in New York City. And as long as Finbar's last walk on that fateful morning in Florence when the world shook itself free of the thing he loved the most, and he retired into oblivion to feast on his own heart, among other things.

I sling it round my shoulder and I climb the south side of our house to the roof, where I will tie the rope from our chimney to the twins' chimney. There, I will take my first walk, a humble length, but in the doing I will be feathered like Finbar, with the world below me, an open mouth, surrounded by water it cannot yet see. And you will clap so loud, a *racket*, that it will be, amidst streetcars, slurs, barrel fires, bottles smashed, sirens, the only sound that will reach me thirty feet above the ground. No matter how far you have gotten, even if you are clinking bronze mugs with Finbar, both of you in your overcoats despite the air outside being, you both agree, *sultry*, I will hear you. Your two half-ruined hands coming together as cymbals.

Our last night together, before we fished in the sideways rain, I did a handstand on a crane, hundreds of feet above a construction site on Lake Shore, just east of Bathurst, and below, you marched the mud, you snorted and paced, a penned-in rodeo bull, eyes on me, a speck, a balancing speck, and suddenly you hollered, 'A daredevil, an aerialist, a miracle!' like a great audience was gathering and they were hungry. *Pow pow.* You startled me with your cry, I tipped, a silver needle, speedometer, but I steadied myself, my white nightgown another skin, folded loose and sodden against me. My palms firm, they pressed down against the wet metal, making my stamp, my future.

But for a moment I imagined myself, barrelling toward the ground like the woman in the photograph did, barrelling so fast that even if you did want to catch me, you couldn't.

Partway to the roof, I crouch in front of Immaculata's bedroom window. Between her thumb and forefinger, she holds a mouse by the tail. The mouse is as big as her tongue and brownish. If the mouse were a girl, she would be called plain. Immaculata pets her and places her on her stained handkerchief. Another common lump gone. Immaculata does not feel sorrow. She feels only curiosity, clean curiosity.

She fills a glass jar with rubbing alcohol. I watch her breathe in the smell of it, a pure antiseptic, unabashed. She is grateful for the authority of a solvent. She holds the mouse up by her tail and drops her into the clear liquid. A small splash. She puts the lid on the jar. There is no sorrow around death for Immaculata. It is only the place where she has the most questions. She lowers her body to the floor and stares, in line with the jar, as if wishing the mouse's dull brown eyes for her own. The mouse spins weightless.

I pull myself onto Mink's windowsill. She stands erect in her nighttime robe rubbing cold cream into her face, which is now a white mask. And then she does two things I have never seen her do before: she pulls out her teeth and she lifts a wig off her head. Underneath, she has a few strands of long grey hair. Without teeth, her face sinks inward. Without hair, her scalp is a shine, the last strands, crooked and desperate. Cracks on a shell. She could burst apart.

My rope falls to the ground. And I fall, fast after it.

My breath in pinpoints. Eventually it matches Immaculata's, calm as a tidal pool.

We sit at the edge of my bed, the rope still around my neck. A collar, brittle and sure, its bite rises red on my skin. 'Don't you dare.' She smells like antiseptic. When she bolted into my bedroom, I was hanging from the rafter, my body kicking, a kipper on the end of a line. I will have a bruise on my stomach from where she charged me.

Immaculata's braids came undone in the struggle. Looking at her now, the colour of wax, I see that she has grown her hair to cover her face. Not because it is ugly, no, but because it has that quality of belonging to another world and she is tired of uninvited eyes. Her beauty has pried her open long enough. Her cheeks are Paleolithic slabs, her hair red as warning, her eyes: ink wells. She is betrayed by their depths, and tries to coat them, blinking back indifference. 'Don't you dare, Euge.' She says it again, hard. With a period at the end of the sentence. Suddenly full of punctuation. *Death for life. A clean trade.*

You taught me how to tie a noose, and after you did, you said to me, 'Unlearn that, unlearn that right now, Eugenia!' But I never forget anything.

Mink appears in the doorway, her arms up against its sides, the threshold of a saloon. She is naked and sweating. Her breasts hang shallow. Her belly is round and small like the tip of a helmet. She gives the impression that she has been running for years, reached her destination and forgotten what it is that she wanted. She looks at us as though she has never seen us before. She does not come toward us in measured steps. She does not chide us. She does not hold our faces to hers and make promises about the future. She does not make us hot drinks. She does not cry. She barely interrupts this moment that is a lifespan in itself. Instead, bald and toothless, her face buried under a thick coat of white cold cream, she says, 'How do you even know he was your father?' and then, for one last time, she rises up onto the tips of her toes, those sharpened points, turns, opens the winter closet, pulls out a brown fur coat and a pink toque and makes her naked way down the hall and down the stairs. Too late, Immaculata says, 'Where are you going?' And then, never forgetting her manners, 'Good night.'

We listen to Mink's footsteps fade. The retreat of an intruder. A perfect stranger. The click of the front door. The whine of the engine. We look out the window. The car pulls away. The sign still there: *with my daughter*. Mink is gone. We are safe. For now. We laugh. We laugh in shudders and balls, heaps and chokes, spores caught on the wind.

Mink leaves her hairbrush behind.

As though performing for my stare, Immaculata's body begins to exaggerate itself, a swan attacking. In a shock, her red hair turns milk-white and her bones sling through her, multiplying themselves, an eerie mathematics. Immaculata does not groan or cry but watches intently, the spectator to a race, as she embodies her final transfiguration. She is a giantess with the appearance of a child bride. Her white dress is now shockingly short, pulled tight against her, a bandage. I realize it was this that stopped people in the street. They could sense that her form could shift. They would not so much watch Immaculata as they would be watchful in her presence, unsure of what they might witness; she could have a fit and lash out or bite her tongue or fly. Whereas, if she could, she would drop herself into a jar filled with clear liquid and spin weightless for the white noise of eternity, under a box spring, in a house soon to be entirely abandoned, a world abandoned of eyes.

And then it is my turn. I grow. It is the sound of a heavy gate being opened, hands crowded against it, pushing. Then there is a loud crack – lightning cleaving a tree, and briefly the smell of burning. Immaculata is transfixed, her mouth a loose zero. She directs me to my door frame, presses my ruler against the top of my head, lilts, 'Don't move,' measures and makes a mark. Three inches. She adds an exclamation point and dates it: June 9, 1981. 'Whoa.' She fumbles the ruler; it hits the hardwood floor and with everything around it – clay pipe stems, snow globes, my neat piles of feathers and shells, my owl lamp, my black corduroy dress – it is instantly a remnant of a previous life. My room smells like storage unit. I do too.

As we fall asleep on my bed, curling into the shape of fiddle-heads for the night to pry apart, Immaculata wrapped around me, stiff and suited, this is what she tells me, her voice a balm, her mouth suddenly full of hard stops: 'Take a duck. Pull her feathers. Save for the head and neck. Baste her with butter. Make a fire around her. Not too close so that she chokes. She will run, walk and fly meekly amidst the flame. Cloistered in a roast, her heart and head will thirst. Wet her with a sponge. When she begins to stumble, she is quite cooked. Present her before your guests. She will cry as you cut into her and be almost completely eaten before she dies. It is mighty pleasant to behold!' Immaculata twines a strand of her floor-length white hair around my wrist. It is thick as fishing line. And then she says, 'Meat is said to be more tender if it is made to suffer first.'

I wait for her to say something more but she doesn't.

two

I^t all started with Sudbury.

June 1, 1980. One year and seven days before you duct-tape this
note to your studio door,

> *gone to save the world*
> *sorry mink,*
> *immaculata,*
> *sorry*
> *yours*
> *sheb wooly ledoux*
> *asshole*

and leave us with fish (mostly bone), Mink is called away to shoot
a film. When she gets the call, she exclaims, 'Oh,' as though something agile just flew up her skirt.

It is a B movie. Mink used to be Joan of Arc. She used to
be Masha. She used to be Ophelia. Now she will be in Sudbury
for seven nights shooting *Murder in the Tundra*. She shows me the
whites of her eyes whenever she says *Sudbury*. She will stay in a
college dormitory. It will smell of sneakers and spaghetti, rank
as leftover childhoods. She will sleep on a cot under a poster of
a fantasy girl who is not her. The walls will be white cement
blocks. There will be fire routes everywhere. She will pack her
own bedding. And her robes, morning and night, which she will
wear while walking to the communal bathroom. Everyone will
fall in love with her. Of this, she is almost sure.

Mink is to play the dim-witted but kinky Austrian prioress
of a motel named the Lay-He-Ho and she must have sex with
a demented dictionary salesman who is passing through town.

His name is Laird. But because of her station in life, she must call him Herr Laird.

'We all have our station in life,' Mink tells me, offering her profile. It should be printed on thousand-dollar bills.

'How true,' I say, not offering mine.

Mink hands me the script. She wants to rehearse. I rifle through the pages. It is mostly about dying and disrobing. When I remark that the film calls for full nudity, she slaps her thigh, a prize cow.

'But aren't you being exploited?' I ask.

'Pshaw. Doing nudity is high praise, Genie. High praise.' She says *high praise* like it is contraband. Like it is what everybody wants but only a few know how to find. This was not always the case. Once, when Mink had not had a call for months, she asked me if I thought she could pass for my sister. I said yes. My lie became every lie that had ever been told to her.

'Swear on Sheb's life.'

It was up to me to undo them all. I couldn't. Mink kicked a cupboard door closed and told me that her industry did not know what to do with her as she got older and so it had abandoned her. Then she pulled on her cheekbones, 'Aging is like misfiring,' and left the room, tipping on her heels.

There was a production of *La Finta Giardiniera*. Your favourite opera. You said, 'Mozart wrote it when he was eighteen. Eighteen, Eugenius. Eighteen.' The final moment of the opera was to be a flock of doves flying high over the audience's heads. They rehearsed with fake doves. On the opening night, they stored the real doves in a net above the stage. When the time came for the doves' flight, they pulled back the net and instead of a flurry of wings, the doves fell dead to the ground. They had been too close to the lights. The heat had killed them. This is what aging is like. You are supposed to be a dove in the air but instead you are burned alive. With an audience that, upon seeing you, is horrified.

More exercises. More cold cream for Mink.

We rehearse. Mink mostly says, 'Oh yes, Herr Laird.' I play Herr Laird. I ask for a room key and then as I am unpacking my dictionaries I go demented like someone has poured hot grease into my ears. This is when I dial for room service. Mink arrives with a cart of dishes under domes. I make small talk until she undresses and then Mink, naked, says, cueing me, 'Stab me, stab me,' under her breath. I can't.

She looks at me. I am ferocious, a barbarian. I am ruining the scene. And then I realize that she is still in character. *Tickety-boo.* Mink enacts her mortal wounds without my help. She runs behind her bedroom curtain and she screams. She yodels a bit and then dies. As she clutches her throat, her frayed jugular winks blood at the cosmos. She swans to the floor. I look at her with frightened curiosity, the way Frankenstein must have watched his monster bloom. She does not blink. I am sure she has stopped her heart. Then she comes to her feet and, with the curtness of a thing snapping shut, she says, 'Scene.'

I wipe my eyes on my sleeve. I applaud. She is Joan of Arc. She is Masha. She is Ophelia.

'You die very well.'

'Thank you.'

Mink curtseys and then she puts herself back together, like a magician's assistant, not sawed in half after all.

'Is there an android in your movie?'
'Not this one.'

I sit on Mink's bed. A double with a dark throw. Three mattresses. I wilt into them, a small shock of milkweed. Her back to me, Mink brushes her hair. 'One, two, three' – steady as a metronome, she counts the strokes under her breath. It falls in glossy switches. Red as embers. Red as Mars. If we were locked in this room until the end of time, all we would do is brush Mink's hair. I might say *chilly* once and then realize that this is beside the point. The point is this: Mink has a silver-handled hairbrush. It is her only heirloom. She says the word *heirloom* as though if she is not careful with it, it will crumble in her mouth and she will cough dust. Like Sheb, Mink was adopted. She does not know her true origins. This makes three things they have in common: feet, sex and question marks. This is why her hairbrush is so important. It is a visit from her ancestors. Every number: mileage covered. The more she counts, the closer they get. 'Forty-nine, fifty.' She puts the hairbrush down. I have question marks too.

'Tell me your beginnings,' I say for the first time.

She trains her eyes on me. They are violet and gold, glistening nuggets. She just plucked them from a dead sailor. From her trunk of faces. 'My mother was an opium addict. My brother terribly ill. A lung disease. We lived by the seaside. There was whisky and whores. My father was cheap. A retired actor. Our maid was stupid. My father was the king of Britain. I had two sisters. They were both treacherous. I was my father's favourite and then he banished me from his kingdom. I was a child prodigy with a hole in my heart. My mother was a statue come to life. She was in love with a man who was haunted by the ghost of his own father. We had a child buried in our backyard. Drowned. My father watched television. My mother turned to God. Our estate was auctioned off. We lived on a cherry orchard. It was cut down. *Que sera sera*. My mother was a witch and full of spells and she drove my father, an artist of some repute and much adored by all, mad, upon which he walked into the forest behind our home never to be seen again. That last part is true.'

I know to never ask her again about her beginnings. So they sit, hot blisters on her skin, never to burst.

Fingers stuck with rings, Mink directs me to her vanity table. She places me, pawn, in front of her, queen. Photographs and dried bouquets crowd the edges of the mirror. The hairbrush is cradled in her hands like it is made of sparrow bones. Will she beat me with it? No. She is trying to even out the attention she expends. She senses a deficit in me and she wants to correct this. Things should be symmetrical. Octagonal. Even love. So she picks me for the hour. She picks me for her riches. 'You're so small, Genie. Some might call it a disadvantage. Even a deformity.' She pairs her face with mine. A rare bird on my shoulder, it could split apart into a swarm. 'I wouldn't. You have your father's face. But you have good skin. My skin. Lit from within. Bet I could find you in the dark.' She straightens. 'Don't look so sad. Sadness will wreck your face. It'll freeze that way.'

Mink touches my scalp. Her fingers are a pitchfork. She pushes my shoulders down. She lifts her one heirloom. It hovers above my head. I worry that it will break when it touches me and that her meagre history will be lost to her forever. It doesn't.

She brushes my hair. It is full of knots and tangles. But Mink ploughs through. *Tickety-boo.*

The first few pulls make me feel seasick, but as she goes on, I hope that she will never stop. With every stroke, she is whispering to me. Grand whispers made of fur and dynamite. *This is where you come from,* she is telling me. *The land of smooth hair. Welcome back, child. You have been away too long.*

I know this much. You told me. She was born here in Toronto and her parents named her Monique. They gave her away. You guess that her mother was probably young, even twelve, and lived in tenement housing and plunged needles into her arms. Mink is a nickname you gave to her. She is adopted by an older couple who dies before I am born. She is their only child. She goes to a private school. She wears a kilt and a blazer and a tie and she is on the swim team. The medley. She knows her lace, her silver and her seams. She goes to dance and piano classes. She has many trophies. Everything in her house is polished. At night, everything shines. When her mother drives through the city alone, she puts a dummy in their back seat to deter kidnappers. That is how rich they are. Everybody wants to take them for ransom money. Still, her parents worry about bills so they keep the house very cold. In the winter, Mink's trophies gather frost. When Mink marries you, an orphan painter from northern Ontario who does not cut his toenails, never uses a napkin and misquotes 'Kubla Khan' (though you were very close to getting it right), her parents disown her. This is why she never speaks about them. This is why she did not go to their funerals. She needed a beast, one who would wrap her in a horse blanket and steal her from her front stoop.

Mink never met her birth mother. According to you, she wanted to remain hidden. Does she live in a bunker and carve the name MONIQUE into the wall over and over again? Are there other women in other bunkers carving names, names that no longer match faces? Somewhere Mink has a mother covered in needles. Somewhere Mink has a mother who could pass for her sister.

She steps back. She laughs. 'You look like a peacock. Like peacock roadkill,' she says. I open my eyes. It's true. She strokes my cheek. Her hand is soft, kelp, and I am the swimmer guessing my way toward shore. I lick my lips. They taste of salt. 'When I get back from Sudbury,' she rolls her eyes, 'I'll take you to the beautician. She'll fix you.' I say, 'That would be nice.' Her smile flashbulbs. I am caught in its frame. She laughs again. I laugh too. Her laughter is so voluminous that I bob inside it. Without warning, she shuts it off. Her eyes go flat. Scene. Too late, too easily overtaken, I am still laughing. I tell her, 'I love your teeth so much.' It is time for her to pack. It is time for me to go. *Stab me, stab me*, I think as I close her door behind me.

June 7, 1980. The day comes for Mink to leave for Sudbury. She gleams like the side of a never-flown airplane. A submarine before it plunges. A revolver. Immaculata and I cannot help but follow her around. She is having a torrid affair with herself. She is full of sideways glances. She calls this *method*. Her bags have been packed for a week. They sit by the front door, hounds panting at the gate. I wonder if they, like her, will break into a sprint.

Mink practices her diction while attending to her toilette and ministrations. She says, 'Red leather yellow leather red leather yellow leather,' over and over again in the Austrian accent required of her. She moves with the deliberation of an empress inside a dark castle – her wrists heavy with gems, beheadings in the basement. And then she repeats, '*Sitzen, liegen, schlafen,*' in different pitches. Immaculata and I are her stunned ladies in waiting. We are bowed. We need aprons and moles. '*Sitzen, liegen, schlafen.*' Mink fixes her hair into place. Her hands are a cursive; the air, lap dogs. She pulls buttons through their holes. '*Sitzen, liegen, schlafen.*' She is already being watched. She has an audience of millions sitting shoulder to shoulder. After the show, she will sign posters of herself. She will look every single one of her admirers in the eye. They will see this as winking. She will be their fantasy girl.

Mink is picked up by a black limousine. Upon seeing the chauffeur, his hunchback frame in a dark suit, looking as though he has been living on arsenic and menthol cigarellos, Immaculata leans into the living room window and says, 'The Grim Reaper,' like she recognizes him and his sallow visage. Like they were intimates and now she is welcoming him home. She knows all of the chains that hang around his neck. One was a gift from her. She has been growing her hair all this time, her teeth turning soft, thinking only of him. And now he has come. For Mink. Immaculata's eyes water; they have been stamped upon by tiny hooves.

Before Mink leaves, she says to us, 'This was always my dream, to be a travelling showgirl.' She sings one note. 'Ra.'

'But aren't you coming back?' asks Immaculata.

'Ra.'

The chauffeur puts Mink's suitcases and hat box into the trunk. He holds the door open. Immaculata knocks on the window. Thinking the knock is for her, Mink glances over at us, her eyes not quite settling on our eager outlines. She opens her mouth and then closes it. Whatever it is she was going to say to us she decides to save for herself. She is taken away, the black limousine vanishing into traffic on the Gardiner. Immaculata's brow beads with sweat. She wipes it away with a stained white handkerchief, which she tucks back under the lace sleeve of her dress.

We look at the old photographs of Mink lining the hallway. They are from what Mink calls *her prime*. The days before we were born. When she was a dove. Immaculata says, *sotto voce*, 'The death of a star.'

Not one for farewells, you finally emerge from your studio. Once Mink is on the highway, in the fast lane, her window rolled down, scarf flying out, a tongue pointed at the wind, her hair unpinning itself, a jellyfish, she practices her death yodel, screaming it at the oncoming traffic. Cars pile up and crunch like a game played for Titans.

You are stock-still for a second, listening for rodents in the walls. Not hearing any, you waltz me briefly. Immaculata blushes the colour of nipples. You pull a piece of crumpled paper and a twenty-dollar bill from your pocket. 'I'm a twenty-dollar man,' you say, and you clap the money into Immaculata's hand. Before she can leave through the front door, you squint at her: 'A happy hunting ground filled with bushwhackers, horse thieves, whisky peddlers, counterfeiters, marauders that'll kill you for a hatband.' You are quoting *Hang 'Em High*. Then you bite the air in my direction. We are a triumvirate now. You send Immaculata to Mister Smoke and Milk with a list entitled: *provisions*. Mink will be away for one week.

provisions
potatoes
white bread
white sugar
white cheese
milk
bacon
hot dogs
margarine
newspaper
lottery ticket
surprise treats (one each)

Above the list, you draw a monk in flight with an enormous penis. We have seen you naked. We know what penises are.

'I am thankful I do not have one,' Immaculata confided after our first viewing.

'Still I admire it such as one might a handsome but mysterious pet.'

'It's probably the same as having a place in the country.'

'Or a separate apartment.'

'With no furniture.'

'Empty but beloved.'

'And you visit it sometimes.'

I am perplexed by the list. So is Immaculata. Her face is that of a nun buying underwear. This is not your version of how to feed oneself in the universe. I have stood by your side too many times while you and your special men palm the heads of cabbage like lost sons. But Immaculata's desire to fulfill orders has overrun her puzzlement. Before I can inquire, she has already made her way to the store. Still in her nightgown, she is fragile, a sleepwalker in the daytime. Her skin is translucent as tracing paper. I see her tiptoeing along a ledge, pigeons at her feet, pollen and the uninvited eyes hanging heavy around her, toothbrushes in their pockets, lullabies rotating in their heads.

St. Joseph of Cupertino was nicknamed Open Mouth because he was retarded and his mouth hung open. Many bugs, too many to count, were caught, trapped and swallowed by him. This is a horror for any Jainist, who wears a mask over his mouth to prevent the needless consumption of winged creatures. The Jainists even have separate headquarters for insects because all things are holy.

I think about living naked in that room full of insects. The sweep of thousands of wings against my skin, eyelashes and skirt hems and fitful souls. I would be their landing place. I would lie on the floor and be so covered in creatures that when Mink, frantic with her suitcases and hat box and fantasy-girl posters of herself, having travelled the globe to find me, walked into the room, she would not be able to see me, so hidden would I be by wings.

Open Mouth could fly. Which means he caught an excess of bugs. All of them, airborne together. When in flight, Open Mouth brought passengers: townspeople, the sick, stray dogs and less talented monks. He carried an eighteen-foot cross along for one flight and a sea urchin for another. It is said that it was not faith so much as lust that made St Joseph fly. His mouth was open for Mary more than anyone else. Lust makes you levitate. Lust gives you the better view. While others have to imagine the tops of trees, the tops of towers, the tops of heads, not so St. Joseph. I conclude that he is your erect monk.

Immaculata comes home with the groceries and, as instructed, surprise treats: a mousetrap for her, a pair of oversized sunglasses for me and a pink cigar wrapped in 'IT'S A GIRL!' for you. You love my sunglasses. When I put them on, you call me *pet, pixie, petit rêve, plaything in the everlasting sun.* Immaculata keeps the change. I see it poking through her bobby sock. A quarter and some pennies mixed in with her anklebone. Maybe she has a hundred dollars somewhere and she will buy an exotic pet that she will slaughter and stuff and name Véronique.

A ringmaster, you direct us to settle ourselves at the table. We watch you make a *banquet!,* a meal that involves *all the ingredients!* You puff on your cigarette, cheeks an accordion, the kitchen overcast with smoke. With much clapping, you spread the meal out. It is finger food for freaks: a giant bowl of cereal (the whole box of cereal, the whole carton of milk); potatoes fried and burned in bogs of margarine; hot dog after hot dog smothered in cheese, bacon and white sugar, each wrapped in a slice of white bread. You say, excitedly, 'What is the point of a bun when you get more out of a bread slice? They sell the bun as though it is a higher version of the bread slice. If you look at the bread slice, actually look at the bread slice, look at the wraparound, the innate wraparound of the bread slice, it is a miracle. It is really a matter of volume, girls, a matter of volume. I hate the bun. The bun is a lie, and losing the war to the slice in this household one hot dog at a time. Breadwinner, bread-winner, breadwinner, say it with me now.'

'Breadwinner. Breadwinner. Breadwinner.'

You are being ironic. You are imitating the 'Everyman' to get us thinking. To make a point about 'Consciousness' and 'Content.' You always write in lower case, but you speak in upper case. This is a sermon. It could last for hours. It could last for days. If you were in a pulpit, you would break it. You always need more space. A mountain range. A perfect meadow. The moon. Here, there is too much to trip on. What you would call junk. Kitchen chairs and carpets and doors. The dish rack. The lamp. Mink's water-skiing photo. You turn the floor to splintered glass and chipped wood with every point. Debris and dots of blood rise on our bare arms and cheeks. The world is never big enough for you. You are the mouse squirming in the tight throat of a cobra. You are always the one to lose at musical chairs. We are not afraid. If one of us interrupted your sermon and said, 'Hold me,' you would. And you would do it so well that we would wish you stood on our street corner with a sign that read FREE HUGS and that all the sorrowful people with sleep lines on their faces could go to you and be mended by your good grip.

At your behest, Immaculata and I read the backs of the cereal box and the plastic tombs that held the hot dogs. We lean our noses into the cartons and smell the antibiotics in the milk. While we run the sugar through our fingertips, you tell us about rats fed with sugar water. The rats binge and become addicts. Without their sugar water, the rats go into convulsions. You scratch your ears, a sugary rat, and then you suddenly stop your sermon, say, 'There,' and take my photograph: nightgown, sitting at the kitchen table, elbow propped against it, one hand holding up my chin, I am looking out the window at a squirrel with a shred of paper in his mouth. He is scampering up the trunk of a tree and then tightroping a branch. He drops the paper and feeds on a nut. His motions are private and subtle as snacking in church. He looks at me. His eyes are jet black and in that jet black, they are the eyes of every animal. I get it. The world is made up of winged creatures and we are the open mouth.

I make a sign. I staple it to a two-by-four. I picket in front of Mister Smoke and Milk.

DON'T EAT THE HOT DOGS

People walk by. Some of them scowl. I imagine them full of pig hearts and pig kidneys and pig livers. I imagine them full of squirrels. I take to wearing a black armband. And sometimes I sleep with a mask over my mouth.

Over the course of the week, the banquet hardens and congeals. Immaculata has shown me photographs of the dead in various poses, supine and not. The banquet takes on the features of the embalmed. We do not touch it. We are of course forbidden. Immaculata says that we are getting arsenic cheeks. Her diagnosis: absence of meat. Meanwhile, pantomime of a man reading the newspaper, you read the newspaper over and over again in crisp folds and squares, smoke sometimes catching the edge of a section, Immaculata there, bare-handed, to put it out. You cut out the birth announcements and add them to your collection. You say, 'I love beginnings!' with every one you snip. You do not go into your studio once. Mink would have called this *unheard of.*

Mink calls us one night. We gather around the speakerphone like she might be full of cowboy poetry. Instead, in her Austrian accent, she tells us stories about her days on set. There are people in the background with whom Mink exchanges jovialities, her pitch that of a bar wench, every passerby her peg-legged customer. Mink tells Immaculata that she can see her doing this one day because of her *schönheit,* her *God-given beauty.* Immaculata dips her head camel-low, imagining herself in an evening dress, coiled in thick rope, tugging this way and that, a black steam engine smoking toward her.

Dishes clutter the sink and the bathtub. The cats move in, their fur floating like dandelion seeds. We drag our mattresses into the living room and sleep there in front of the fireplace. You throw out the toaster, saying angrily, 'Somewhere there is an island full of these things.' The couch is next. The curling iron last. We do not change out of our nightgowns. Even when we paint the hallways with bold slogans:

Gluten dulls the children!
Beware the white bread!
Milk kills!
Luddites are our friends!

I get used to Mink's absence. We all do. And so it is jarring when the Grim Reaper brings her back and she smells of menthol and she looks for the toaster and the couch and the curling iron, and she sees us, her chalk-coloured children, our matted hair, the paint on our arms and nightgowns spotted and striped, a different species entirely, and she sees the meal laid out before us, palliative, and the ruined kitchen and the slogans, cats bawling at her ankles. She drops us in the bathtub, and then she says to you, 'How was your week?' and then she flicks your forehead between the eyes. You flinch. Her touch is a starter's pistol. You do not answer her. Instead, you shuffle her question through your faculties. She has interrupted a delicate state of being. And then she says, 'Have you lost your mind?' and, with that, I think you do.

Soon after, you take me to Our Spot by the Lake for the first time.

I wake to you standing above me, grinning. You should have bird feathers between your teeth. A thermos of coffee and a bag of worms in your hands. Apples in your suit pockets making you the many-breasted Artemis, goddess of the beasts. Boots grinding the carpeted floor, you are flinging sparks. *Secret.* And suddenly we are on your bicycle and we are, with your fist in the air, heading southeast *to fish and to make fire!*, our house and the life that we stage within it shrinking behind us to a dot on a map – instantly, the Old World. How far will we go? The Scarborough Bluffs? The Orient? And will we ever go back? Or should I start to memorize my mother's face now? My sister's? Every night I ask myself this question, and every night we return home, smelling like fire.

I sit myself on your handlebars, my back to you, contracted into the shape of a snapdragon. Slicing through traffic: our bravery game. I punch out the lenses of my oversized sunglasses so I can feel the wind whistle through my eyes.

On your bicycle, we are flying. In my socked feet and nightgown, I stand up on your handlebars, the prow of a ship heading into the great unknown, and I climb onto your mile-wide shoulders, can see the next continent, hands cupped around the top of your head, a crown, fingers burrowing into knotted tufts of hair, thick and dry, that haven't been washed in weeks. My face is frozen into a smile. Leaves skid the road in green shots. You catch the moon, always heavy in your mouth. You tell me *it tastes like ice and regret.* You tell me *it tastes like liftoff.* You tell me you have tasted everything in your life. Is this true? *Been around the sun fifty-nine times.* Is this true? *Still prefer the dark.* And there on your shoulders, feet dangling down to your blinking belt buckle, in that spine-straight attitude of Finbar's beloved who fell all those mornings ago in Florence, I wave to an imagined crowd. You see them too. And then you introduce me, saying my secret name for the first time. 'Stunt,' you yell it extravagant, 'Stunt.' A word juggled up into the black night. 'Stunt.' I drink it thirstily as a nectar. And unlike Finbar's beloved, I do not fall.

The morning you disappear, Immaculata stands at the end of my bed. She glows, a girl pulled from a marsh. A maiden, ragged and graceful. She should be covered in moths. She should be holding out a pear. Something is wrong, and when something is wrong, it is you. She does not say anything. Instead, she stands with her mouth open. That is where the pear should be. That is where the moths should fly from.

And then, false-starting, she says, 'He.'

There is only one He in our life and He is fixed how gravity is fixed. He is the Law of our Universe.

Mink and Immaculata shuffle from foot to foot like the floor is fiery coals. Immaculata says, 'There is nothing left of him but five fish there is nothing left of him but five fish there is nothing left of him but five fish.' I find your note. It is duct-taped to the inside of your studio door, your own eviction notice, the drawing of the flying monk, his enormous penis, and below, in your ragged script:

> *gone to save the world*
> *sorry mink,*
> *immaculata,*
> *sorry*
> *yours*
> *sheb wooly ledoux*
> *asshole*

'No Eugenia,' says Mink.
'No Eugenia,' echoes Immaculata.

'None.' I round them up. They look at me as if I have nipped their ankles and taken square centimetres of their skin.

Mink has never seen the flying monk. She does not know his significance. Every human being has his own Morse code. Yours was particularly dense. She studied you as one might read the clavicle of a bull, trying to divine messages from fractures and patterns. But to no avail. She did not live in your age. She did not have that skill. I did. I would know.

I read the note once, roll it between my fingers, a missile, leave the studio and place it on the kitchen table, careful, it may go off. Five fish are fanned out there. Fried in butter. The pan is still on the stove. I touch it. A blister forms on my fingertip. I kick up my chin, feel my hair down my back, brambles, and shake my head, the horse before the race.

Your bicycle.
I run to the window.
Your bicycle.
Gone.

The apple tree has been plucked bare. I run to your bedroom, spare change gone, matches too. Did you kiss me while I slept? I touch my mouth. Yes. I look in the bathroom: toilet seat left up. Open the top drawer of your dresser: my baby hair is gone, that black tuft between the tie clips, single socks, handkerchiefs, leather boxes, pencils, French cigarettes and a photograph of you in your suit, in a rooming house, canvases lined up against the wall, attentive, waiting, and you, pretending to sword-fight them with a brush, cigarette dancing in your mouth, everything dancing for you, the world an instant tango. *Huzzah*, I hear your voice, *huzzah*. I run faster. The same route: the kitchen, the frying pan, the window, the bedroom, my mouth, the bathroom, the dresser, the kitchen, the frying pan, the window, the bedroom, my mouth, the bathroom, the dresser, the kitchen, the frying pan, the window, the bedroom, my mouth, your dresser – until a new part of me is lanced into being, red splotches burst on my neck making meteors of my skin, I beat them back. A brush fire. To put it out, you have to axe the roots.

three

It smells like butter and crematorium. It smells like melted dolls.

Immaculata whistles in her sleep. If she sleeps. Of this, I have never been sure. She does not whistle songs, but whistles as though she is calling for something, for someone. Probably the dead. So marooned is she on the other side of the River Styx. The summoner. I crash mercifully against the rocks. I am whistled awake.

With her call, the sun rises, swelling the room and wresting my eyes open. They are hard-boiled eggs. I have not really slept for a year, with you always shaking me out of it, your fresh tobacco breath, *secret*. *Secret*, I would repeat, touching my heart or my throat, fingers a cuff.

'Good morning, Eugenia.'

'Good morning.'

Immaculata sits beside me, upright, pew posture. She watched me through the night, the bitten edges of my sleep, the hum of my breath, my stiff body an ache, having broken through the quiet of our world, taking floorboards, stained carpets and set tables with me, a wig, false teeth and a note duct-taped to a door. A skydiver falling fast. If I asked Immaculata, she would tell me what I dreamed about. But I don't. I already know. In four days, I have become a person with only one dream.

We get up, look for Mink, knowing that she is gone, the world her pageant. Still, there is effort in our search. We scream her name loudly; our house is a black ocean and she is adrift within it. We look in closets. In the basement. We pull back curtains and covers. We open and close doors, the refrigerator. We check underneath beds — every moment, a jack-in-the-box. She took nothing with her save the fur coat, the pink toque and the car.

'She didn't leave a note,' says Immaculata, deflating.

'I wonder if she has already forgotten our names.'

'I wonder if she has already forgotten her name too.'

'Maybe this is why she won't answer our screams.'

'Maybe.'

'Because she's forgotten who she is.'

'Maybe she's still here somewhere and we're scaring her silly.'

'Mink doesn't get scared.'

'True.'

'She wouldn't forget that.'

All the lights are off. We enter the bathroom, its surfaces still in a sweat from the night before. We flick on the overhead light; it twitches into brightness. We bend into the sink together and scrub our faces, and it is then that the mirror delivers the final evolutionary fear: in the night, we have doubled in age. We are eighteen. Instantly and thoroughly, eighteen. Our mouths are crowded with teeth, my black eyes and bruised neck healed. We lean into our reflections and trace our new faces, the old ones tucked inside them, Russian dolls. Our jaws are strong, our cheeks less full. Faint lines have formed, shading, around our eyes and our lips, our loose grip on childhood now gone. Were we asleep for nine years? We turn on the radio. No. It confirms that this is the fourth day, the fourth day since you disappeared. June 10, 1981. The fourth day of Sheb Departed. The world remains the same. We are the ones changed.

We examine our shapes. With Immaculata's height came curves. She stands sideways to the mirror and then spins slowly, a figurine on a cake. 'Whoa.' She is impressed. I am too. If I had a glass of something, I would spill it. She has breasts that bounce like she is riding in an apple cart, and a down bustle for a bottom. It is as though the magi were here and they were erotic-minded, visiting her, their eastern star, with curves hidden in their bulky coats, bestowing them to those willing eyes in the hay. I am still flat from the side, a pencil drawing, contourless. The shape of a coffin. Sawed straight. Standard Eugenia. My magi, my heat lamp, a thousand miles gone.

We eat cake left over from the funeral. Nuts and cherries. It tastes smoky. Flo.

'I bet they went in opposite directions,' Immaculata says gravely, a beginner detective, mouth white with icing sugar.

'I bet you're right.'

'I bet they don't intend to reunite.'

'No.'

'Their only true commonality was lovemaking.'

'And, in turn, us.'

'They packed hastily and badly, which reflects a lack of fore-thought, and which tells us that this was not a scheme long in the hatching, but rather the directionless instincts of lunatics suddenly freed from an asylum.'

'Not that we were an asylum,' I remind her.

'No. Not that we were an asylum. They loved us, Eugenia.'

'If that's what that was.'

'That's what that was.'

My jaw hurts. Immaculata grips it in one of her hands, which is now more like a paw, a paw that could catch salmon and break necks.

'Though they have forsaken this love.' She softens. 'And we

are not going to live in the hopes that this love, like them, will come back. If we do, we too will be barefoot and walking the streets without identification. We must agree to belong only to each other, to never speak their names, and in so doing, to do what they have done to us – to root them out from behind our eyes. Promise, Eugenia. Promise.'

'No.'

'Yes.'

'No.'

'Yes.'

'No, I'm too old for that.'

We cover the funeral cake we cannot finish and put it back in the fridge, wash our dishes and leave by the front door, Immaculata tripping over her feet and hitting her head on the frame. I tuck the box of matches you gave to me into my pocket and I sling Marta's rope around my shoulder.

But first we spend a moment looking at Mink's wig. It is very fine. We stroke it. Its red is a finality. The velvet curtain. An ending. Precisely what you, even after Mink's toothbrush, will not give over. But this was Mink's way. As she was haunted by nothing, she does not haunt. Whereas you lurk here, your presence a gauze that has draped itself over everything. Our life, a cottage closed for the winter. Water turned off. White sheets on the furniture, shut eyes.

I read your note one last time. Is there something I missed? The letters are short and shaken. You pressed down so hard, bits of pencil fleck the page silver. You wrote it on a scrap of newsprint. The birth and death notices. From the back of the sports section. *I love beginnings!* I lift it to my nose. It erupts. Unwashed man skin, old smoke, cat, wet wool, apple.

> *gone to save the world*
> *sorry mink,*
> *immaculata,*
> *sorry*
> *yours*
> *sheb wooly ledoux*
> *asshole*

You did not write my name because you did not want to distract me with it. You wanted me to study the drawing. The drawing is what counts. The drawing is the clue. The flying monk is not St. Joseph of Cupertino as I had thought, but Finbar. I. I. Finbar Me the Three Handsome Funambulist and Colossal Menagerie. Finbar in his black tights and his leather shoes. Finbar who could not fall.

I hear the slam of our mailbox. Look out the window. The postman. He wears postman shorts. His legs are wishbones. His face is the face of a man who has just learned that there are no fairies.

'Just a minute,' I say to Immaculata and I sprint to the door panther-fast. She cannot, with her new limbs, keep up. 'Wait. Wait,' she pleads, collapsing in a lanky pile near the stairs.

It is a letter. Addressed to me. My first. *Ms. Eugenia Ledoux.* The handwriting, not yours.

I hear Immaculata come to her feet in her too-small white slippers and lumber along the hallway, using the walls for balance, the mariner battling smoke and fog. I stuff the letter into my suit pocket just as she arrives beside me. In the doorway, she looks trapped, too exotic for this place.

'What? What did you find? Did Mink leave a note after all?'

Almost telling her everything — the nights by the lake, my feats, the flying monk, Finbar in photographs flashing his white teeth like sticks of dynamite, the air picking him clean — I say, as tall as her new breasts now, 'No. Nothing.' In that small utterance, that single word, I see for the first time how much I need, how much I love, a secret. And with it, I look up and I begin to memorize my sister's aging face.

'Let's go.' The letter thumps in my pocket, a tantrum. Immaculata stalls. 'Let's go.' I say it again, insistent, our house now taking on the sonority of a cave. I lean into my sister. Her hipbone points sharp like an arrow, north. And then, as you and Mink did before us, we leave. Only we leave together. And we, white dress and black suit, look newlywed.

The house next door is burned down. Its black frame stands naked and quivering, a thing shorn. No walls. No doors. There is a hole in the roof. Inside, embers sputter and hiss. If it rained, it would sound like a den of snakes. A spoon. A child's purple sweater. A television slurred across a table. The first-aid kit. This is all that is left. The rest is charred ruins. Coal sandcastles, black hoodoos still smoking. They slope and point, broken teeth, the twins' faces carved into every surface. It is now, in disaster, that God is an artist. There is a small crowd gathered beyond the yellow tape, taking photographs, the cuffs of their pants blackening with ash. They don't even speak to each other. Mink would have studied the misfortune too.

The twins decided, *against good judgment*, to make pastry for us in the middle of the night. Now they have to wear tight white nets to keep their skin on. When they heal, their faces will be pulled and uneven, smeared with egg whites left there by a cook, half-asleep, to glaze and congeal. Mr. and Mrs. Next Door *have had it*. So the twins have been sent to the suburbs to live with their grandmother who cannot tell them apart so she uses only one name for both of them. Eventually, they do too.

Their grandmother has a one-bedroom apartment, thirty-five storeys up, that looks over a highway and then onto a cemetery. By nighttime, she jokes about the cemetery. On her small balcony she has put a television and hung a flag so weather-ruined, the country is unreadable. There, she watches *her shows* in a housecoat, purse clutched to her chest. She falls asleep, head hanging down. Hair, cobwebs. When the twins wake her to carry her to her bed, their favourite activity, the housecoat slippery, the ankles and wrists too, she pulls them close – soup, baby powder – and whispers, 'When can I go?' 'Never,' they whisper. 'You have to stay here with me,' convincing her that there is only one of them and that she is seeing double.

While Mrs. Next Door walks the debris of their home with the strain of a woman trying not to break anything, we meet the twins' father in the driveway. His eyebrows and eyelashes are singed hay-yellow. He is wearing blue pyjamas. They are threadbare and need mending. His body hair pokes through them, thick as quills. Mr. Next Door coughs a bit, and then he asks, 'What will become of the house?' It is the first time he has ever spoken to us. His voice is mellifluous, pure. It has never been used. If he wanted to read to me for an entire day, in the dark corner of a strange room with nothing else in it but a hobby horse, I would let him. 'We don't know,' says Immaculata. 'We haven't decided.'

Mr. Next Door motions for us to follow. We do. To his hatchback, a peeling dwarf beside him. He opens the trunk. Pop. And pulls out a black suitcase. He flicks it open, covertly, like it is a music box with a wind-up spinning girl. It is full of money. Neat stacks of it. So much, it must be fake.

'Is it real?' I ask, recalling his photocopier scent, seeing him alone in a dank basement, making money, the photocopier light rolling over his face all day, flashbulbs. 'It is,' he says, not lying. He is a man whose failure came for him too young. It hunted him and it shot him down. He blinks, full of dusted-over fantasies. 'I keep my valuables in the trunk,' he adds, flicking the suitcase closed and handing it to us. There is nothing else there. No ruby pinkie rings, no yearbooks. No wife and no twins.

Immaculata takes the suitcase. Surprised by the heft of it, she steadies herself. The bricks of money too much to tuck into her bobby sock.

'You'll find it spotless.'

'Thank you.'

'There's leftover cake in the fridge.'

'Great.'

'It's got nuts in it.'

'No problem.'

'And the bathroom light works, just give it some time.'

'Every house has its quirks.'

'That's our only one.'

I hear a dull chatter. I look back at the house. Termites. They are taking to the wood. They waited for us to leave and, now that we are gone, generations of them are building nests and tunnels. Termites have a king and a queen and they have workers. The workers can feed each other, freeing the parents from this task, allowing the colony to grow, to grow so vastly that it can devour an entire house, slowly winning it over, like children desperate to impress.

Immaculata, not turning around, says, mouth suddenly full of shelves and sharp turns, 'I won't miss it.'

'I will.'

{ POSTCARD FROM OUTER SPACE }

astronaut looking for the following signs:
pay phone.
gents.
rest stop
all-day breakfast.
open.
eugenia stunt ledoux.
one mile ahead.

Clotilda and Yufeng's house is for rent. The sign is speared into the grass, a javelin. So is skinny Selene Valadan's. Her laundry line pulled down and, with her children, disappeared. So is Tuberculosis Flo's. The houses are empty, their occupants long vanished and, in their stead, other people, perfect strangers, mill on the lawns. Clumped together in a garden party, a fake fruit bowl, gleaming baubles, they are prospective renters, notepads in hand, necks craned. Under the sky so blue above them, they appear to have been shined. The neighbourhood raccoons should bite their calves and pull them from their reverie.

Zee Mute's silver car is gone, and he, somewhere, takes a turn too fast, thinks *smithereens*, his eyes part-closed, yelling out the refrain that he has finally memorized. He is proud. He wishes to be held tight. He wishes to be heard.

There must have been moving trucks through the night, their red lights blinking, sirens without sound, conversationless men, loads stacked on their backs and shoulders, short of breath, the sweat on their foreheads like bubble wrap, tracking dirt in and out of these houses, these houses that sit like picture frames waiting to be filled again.

Elsie is dead. Her magazine collection pulls against garbage bags hoisted by distant relatives, their weak, cold arms, confused scowls on their faces. She has already been taken away and turned to ashes and placed in a personalized urn. But still there is so much tidying. Like you, she was a collector.

And Marta's house, like the twins', has been chewed through by fire. There is nothing left of it. Only a square black imprint, cinders like ink gone wrong on a page, a messy stamp, one you would want to do over. The papers flying up are crows. I know that she was in it because as an unemployed existentialist she had no reason to leave. She gave me the rope and then she returned to her dark, where she lit a match and she spun with it between her bookshelves, and they spun with her, her last and most steadfast companions.

My eyes are a vinegar sting and my jaw aches against crying. Why does tragedy have to be so thorough? This time it does happen: my face is stuck through with sadness, and it freezes, just as Mink, with her exquisite hair, warned me it would.

U p the street, across from the church and before the mission, at the corner of King and Dunn, lives my last slab of familiarity, Leopold of the Onions. Mink called him *the Malcontent of Mucusville*. His house is not for rent. His house is not burned down. Though he wishes it were. He prays for it, night and day, he prays for calamity. *Let the lake collect itself into a great tidal wave. Let there be a chemical spill that comes up through the drainpipes. Let me be mistaken for a whale and harpooned.* He does drawings of medieval weapons in his notebook, which he keeps tucked, like a filthy magazine, under his mattress. Crossbows and daggers and spiked balls on the ends of sticks that can be whirled above heads like a ceiling fan; he dreams of them making contact.

There are two signs in his window: BEWARE OF DOGS and HELP WANTED. While his front door opens onto our street, the rest of his house sits facing King Street, a busy thoroughfare of traffic and streetcars. The streetcars clang and whine through the night. So do the prostitutes who congregate there. Their offers and grunts, Leopold's only lullaby. He pulls open the slats of his crooked Venetian blinds and watches them. Their movements, stiff and rehearsed, remind him of a construction site. The hoisting, the lifting, the digging, the pecking. They jerk like heavy machinery. Getting the job done. He plans to give them hard hats and safety goggles. He plans to help them form a union. They know him by name. They pinch his cheeks.

Leopold used to come by our backyard to kick rocks in his white marching boots with the red tassels and unravel his soot-smothered world with the ferocity of a forgotten veteran. His life: an ambush. We would listen to him, you and I, struck still. We were his only audience. As he spoke, to show him the effect of his words, you would unbutton your shirt and then you would scratch your skin. His story was written there and it was unbearable. You would scratch your skin until it bled. Until you were a man who had been lashed. And you would shout vows to him, to punish those who hurt him, and to make his life right. Leopold would be jealous. His sadness was so much better worn by you. He felt almost undeserving of it.

Other days, when he showed up, you simply shook your head and closed our door firm and tight, leaving him a specimen petrified against the glass. Once, I heard you talking to one of your special men, and you told him something that Leopold had told you, but you told it as your own. You believed that it was. You mistook everyone's suffering for your own.

As we walk by Leopold's house today, without our identification, but with our shoes on, he knocks quickly on the window. Tersely, he lifts one finger and he mouths, *Wait*. We do. He has had his eyes fixed on the street for days, the four days you have been gone, and he has not blinked once. He opens his door and emerges from a hallway black as tomb.

He is wearing gardening gloves and a wide-brimmed hat to protect his skin from the sun. He carries a bag of onions. That hoary voice, a teenaged seafarer, 'I have a lot of onions.' He hands them to me with the delicacy of a dowry. He smells of sperm and sunblock. His hair falls straight and pink-blond as newborn mice, his teeth giant white blocks, scrubbed headstones. His eyes are intent, wet, the colour of mashed peas.

'You're so sad. I get sadness,' he says.

'Thank you.'

'I am sorry for your loss. It is most difficult for those left behind.' He would have researched what to say. Read about bereavement etiquette at the library. 'My deepest sympathies.'

'Thank you. We need onions.'

'I thought you might.'

Immaculata nods in agreement. She sees Egyptians buried with flowering onions stuffed in their eye sockets and their pelvises, their chest cavities, their ears. They believed the strong scent could resuscitate the dead, that a corpse wearing a garland might gasp. Leopold does a deep bow in Immaculata's direction. It is surprisingly chivalrous and assured. Is he a knight? Does he have cavalry? A chain-mail tunic? He has caught glimpses of Immaculata but never spoken to her. Always in her white dresses, a stray feather, and once, notably, walking the length of our street in her nightgown, her arms full of groceries. He followed her with his telescope, the wind picking up and pressing itself against her. He wished he were the wind. She is someone whom, up close, he cannot believe is real. She is see-through. Words, his only effect, always seemed too base. He turns to me.

'You look the same only different.'

'We know.'

'You've grown old.'

'We're eighteen.'

'How?'

'Grief.'

'I get grief. Have you read Kafka?'

'*The Metamorphosis.*'

'Bingo.' And then, eyeballing us, 'But hey, it suits you.'

'Thank you.'

'Welcome to the club.'

'Thank you.'

'It sucks.'

'You're getting a moustache.'

'Thank you.'

Leopold fingers his upper lip. Goose down. He smiles to himself. Finally, the magi. Just in time. He turns to Immaculata, puffing his chest.

'What a night will do ... So the twins, eh? They have to wear tight white nets over their bodies and faces for a whole year. Their skin will fall off if they don't.' A green bubble bullfrogs from his left nostril. He wipes it away with his T-shirt, which reads ATLANTIS.

'They tried to make pastry, now they have to live in the suburbs.' He sneezes. It sounds like *hatchet*.

'Excuse me. I have a chill.' By way of explanation, 'Delicate constitution.'

'I understand.' Immaculata's first and most miraculous words to him, the ones he has been waiting to hear his entire life.

Emboldened, he goes on. 'Well, really it's a lung disease, but when I use the word *disease*, my mother thinks I'm feeling sorry for myself so she says, "Oh, are you trying to get through to the complaint department? Oh, just hold the line," and then she beeps sporadically and no one ever picks up. I'll die young. Long before her. I'm about halfway through my life. Can I move in? I only have a notebook and an oxygen tank. I call it Leopold Junior because children are the future.' He laughs in excited, lumpy howls.

'We've abandoned camp.'

'Dammit. This life is a curse.' He slams the lawn with his marching boot, barely an indentation, and draws in a thick wet breath. 'One moment please.' Then he coughs. Immaculata is mesmerized, having never heard such a noise. He is a wolf, an infirm. She pictures iron lungs and spontaneous tracheotomies. The word *pleurisy* fireworks across her brain in ornate curlicues. Leopold's lungs are full of sodden garbage, sand and spilled cans. They are a shoreline that has never been raked. 'The air is still smoky,' he says, and with that he walks backwards – hushed, out of a nursery.

Leopold's nose starts to bleed. His fingers bunch around its base. By the time he gets to his house, his hands are streaming with blood. He pulls out a bundle of keys, thick as a caretaker's. He lifts one finger, 'Wait.' We nod. He unlocks the three locks on his front door with great exertion, his arms those of a jerking bird. His world: stubborn clocks, stuck and ungreased. He evaporates behind the door. Immaculata sees him blue as the underbelly of ice, occupant of a rectangular cabinet, toe tagged, rail-thin. She needs a metal bowl and a steaming cloth. She needs him all to herself.

Leopold closes the door quickly behind him as though a fresh litter might follow. Outside, pollen lolls, a yolk. Dandelion heads everywhere. Bloated flies hovercraft. Immaculata traces the air in front of us and, looking at Leopold, says, 'It's summer.' He smells of shaving cream. There are small cuts above his lip. Still in the wide-brimmed hat and gardening gloves, he has changed his T-shirt: EASTER ISLAND. He also wears a leather motorcycle jacket, black with heavy buckles. It hangs on him, a downpour, making him the abandoned frame of an umbrella. He tugs on its cuffs.

'Better.'

'Aren't you hot?'

'No,' he sniffs. 'Yeah.'

'You shaved.'

'I had to. It was ungainly. So. Dig my jacket?'

'It's a bit big for you.'

'I'll fill it out. It's my mother's boyfriend's, Rolf. But I call him Lady Hips. He thinks he's so tough because he has a pet viper but he's got the hips of a lady, makes waffles in his underwear in the mornings, all swishes. Rolf.'

Leopold's mother is a wrestler. She is the colour of Tang. She is built in thick swipes of beef and muscle. Her fight name is Death Trap Susie. The Death Trap is her signature move. It involves a scissor kick and the insides of her thighs. She has two pit bulls, Prince and Princess. They are trained to kill. The dogs spend most of their time chained in the bathroom, climbing each other's hard backs, trembling and salivating. The only one they love is Leopold.

'She dates only guys whose names sound like body functions,' Leopold says. Immaculata laughs, throwing her head back. Her hair parts. The pearl. 'Rolf. He has a truck dealership called Rolf's Wheels. He is all engorged digits. He keeps his particulars at the dealership. Even the viper. Didn't want to feel domestically beholden. "I'm not your father," he said to me the first time he came over. "I know," I said, "I know," and he said, "I'll never be your father," and I said, "I know, Rolf, it's cool."

'The only things he moved into the apartment were dirty bumper stickers. They're everywhere. Like locusts. The mirrors, the toaster oven, my dresser, even my snare drum for marching band which now says on one side, *For a Small Town, This Place Is Full of Assholes*, and on the other side, *If It Swells Ride It*. He sleeps with his gym bag. I think it is filled with suck-candy and ammunition. Mom thinks he's the jackpot. But every time we see a woman, any woman, even if she's elderly and blind, he punches me in the arm. Not when Mom's around. When she is, she's always doing these little claps after he says anything. We're supposed to go to Disneyland this summer, *clap, clap*, but I know I'll get lost or kidnapped. My mother would cry for three days and then feel relieved, having the apartment all to herself. *Clap, clap*. She could drink cocktails with her waffles, which she can't do when I am around because "Oh, I look at her sideways" and "Oh, I'm no fun."' He imitates her voice. It is lower than Rolf's.

'Last year I tried to kill myself but it didn't work. Now I'm studying auto-hypnosis. I dream of invisibility. I want to appear present, hand up, here, but be elsewhere, frothy surf, bird songs. Get it?'

We nod. We do. A raven hops by with a toy in its beak.

Leopold continues, 'The trouble started with Burk the Elf Killer, my mother's boyfriend before Rolf. He would wake me up in the middle of the night wearing a balaclava and think it funny. He was the cat and I was the baby who smelled of milk.'

Immaculata, pleased by this image, prompts Leopold, who has fallen quiet. Her tone appropriate to a wake in a parlour room, she inquires, 'And what happened to Burk the Elf Killer?'

Leopold returns to his story. 'He was a wrestler too. Now he's in traction. So Susie got hungry.'

He growls. I step back. Immaculata steps forward.

'And your father?' she asks.

'He sends me a calendar every year for Christmas and sometimes a toy boat.' We frown. 'But it's a model schooner and made of real wood. He lives on the East Coast. He has three new children and a wife named Debdeb. I've never met them. My mother thinks it's for the best. That he's gone. He pays for my schooling, but what's the point, I just get knocked out on the playing field and left for dead. They call me Snot Smurf. Even the gym teacher. So I haven't gone for a year. I spend the money on T-shirts. What about the forgotten people? What about them?'

He sings the question. And then he is his own backup singer: 'Who?'

Leopold looks at Immaculata. 'I'm growing my hair.'

'That's nice,' she says.

'Like an infidel.'

'You could disappear,' I suggest.

'No. I can't. My mother last night was like, "Oh, why can't you just macramé or something you're just staring staring staring," but I was like, "At least I'm in the marching band." Later today, she will tan in her sports bra and matching underwear with an emergency blanket under her chin while listening to her shower radio and drinking raw eggs. I tried to drown myself in the kitchen sink. Lady Hips found me. Now he calls me Lee for short.'

Another breath that is drawing lava through a straw. 'Can I watch you do something?'

'Like what?' Immaculata asks.

'Anything. Eat breakfast. Hang from the ceiling. Build a bird bath. Anything.' We look at each other. Leopold offers, 'I could put a table here and say I'm a mind reader.'

'But you're not a mind reader.'

'Hey, a man has to make a living. Or I could just set up my pup tent. The acoustics are good and I can pretend I'm an anchorite. Want to join?'

Before we can answer, there is a scratching sound from inside his house. Leopold blinks rapidly. He starts to hiccup.

'I forgot to lock them in the bathroom.' He hiccups. 'The dogs. When I shaved (*hiccup*), I forgot to put them (*hiccup*) back on their chains.' He lifts his finger. 'Wait.'

He looks up to the bedroom windows. *Hiccup.* Still dark. *Hiccup.* He opens the door. The dogs come outside, look at Leopold and immediately lie down, mouths black with blood, heads burrowing ostrich. Leopold goes inside. He returns moments later with a graveyard face, hiccups gone.

'If our parents aren't parents anymore, do we still have to be sons and daughters?'

Leopold dashes his finger between his eyes until his hand drops, a hero shot in the shoulder. He falls still, unblinking. Immaculata kneels below him. Patiently, she waits for him to wake. Instead, he grows, like Immaculata, uncomfortably tall. He fills out the black leather jacket. They appear to be the twins now, the pale twins, she and Leopold, frail and beautiful lines drawn against the hard surfaces of the world. Set there to be pawed by time. Set there with their white eyelashes.

'You should stay here, Immaculata,' I say. Insects cresting under our feet, the weeds climbing up around us.

'Yes,' she nods, 'I should. With Leopold.' The way she says *Leopold* makes his name longer than it is. Her calling has announced itself.

I give her the black suitcase. She insists on splitting the contents. I stuff my share of Mr. Next Door's trunk money into the bag of onions. Her hair still a rope between us.

Suddenly, Leopold's face takes on the quality of a baby having a nightmare. Immaculata whistles him awake. He looks at her, so thankful. He looks at her and he thinks *forever* and he prays that she thinks it too. He prays that she will say it before he has to. Forever is just too much of a risk to offer first.

Leopold cannot cry. That is why he has so many onions. When he needed to cry to his mother, he would crawl under his bed with a butter knife and slice the onions open and gaze into them until his eyes went watery. When you left, and he had to beg and bleed for days to attend your funeral, she caught him under his bed with the onions. That is why he had the surplus. You left just when he thought of asking you to teach him how to cry. He wanted his hurt to fit him the way it fit you.

Immaculata straightens the cuffs of my suit and runs her fingers down my face, a Braille she can read. We untwine her hair from my wrist. It leaves a red tangle. We hug, buoyant as ocean water, a love surging between us, indelible, my sister's indelible imprint. Feeling the impermanence of all things, the spin of the earth, the pull of a gravity all my own, I move away. She leans into my ear, sugar breath, 'Just don't let it make you love differently.' I look at her bones. Archaeologists will mull over them one day. Even as dust in their hands, they will be able to tell that she was beautiful, oppressively beautiful. *This is how we lived, this is how we lived.*

Her step a lope, she returns to Leopold and the dogs, the pine needles not breaking beneath her feet. Beside them, her face is a burning white candle.

And then, the one word we never heard, 'Goodbye.'

'Goodbye.'

'Goodbye.'

We sew up the moment.

I open the letter.

Ms. Ledoux,

Did your doom-fucked policemen not sing, E minor, 'The gentleman Finbar is dead, dear, the gentleman Finbar is dead'?

The letters are tall and shaken, the last word, *dead*, and its attendant question mark, only partly on the page. His eyes could not see where the page ended and the dresser began. He writes on a dresser. All other surfaces occupied: bottles, nail clippers, rinds of cheese, the stale ends of bread, newspapers, photographs, costume jewellery from the days before her fall. I lift it to my nose. The weather lingers in the paper, the wet weather, the extravagant heavy green. All of his windows must be either open or broken.

I do not see the letter as a caution. He took the time to pull himself from the deep, and he wrote. Oh. And he's not dead. Huzzah. *Huzzah.*

Return address: a po box.

Postage: Canada.

June 10, 1981

Dear I. I. Finbar Me the Three,
I am eighteen now. As I understand it, this has some currency
in your world. Please send directions.

Eugenia

Past the prostitutes, heeled and shimmering, calling me *pussy-cat* and *honeydoughnut* and *angelface*, past the church, past the mission, I mail the letter to Finbar and step off our street. Goodbye, Dunn Avenue. I salute the air. *Pow pow.*

I could live anywhere now. I could dig a hole and hammer in a flag that says *home* and make myself believe it to be true. I could buy a door and stand it up somewhere and write *do not enter* on it and crouch behind it. I could kneel on a family's doorstep, their mismatched furniture on the front porch, and I could beg to be admitted and then add my boots to their lineup of new shoes in the front hall and smell their new food smells and be fed their noodles and sleep with them on mats on the floor and listen to their new parsed breath and try to match it to my own. I could call myself Cheryl. I could never wash again and let myself become feral and walk shirtless through the streets, a filthy mammal who makes terrible scratching sounds and scares women and children. I could freeze to death next winter. I could play the piano and emit the smell of roses. I could decide to wear nothing but skates and only use the word *skate* for everything. *Skate skate skate.* I could tell anyone anything. That I am a sex maniac and I need a frog and a bird fighting in my pants right now. That my father was a welder and beat me with an iron until I was unconscious and then while unconscious he made me banana splits and when I awoke he fed them to me with his shaking hands. *Skate skate skate.* That my mother made me sleep with hundreds of clothespins pinching my skin and called me Laundry Line and she never turned the nickname into a story. I could tell people that I have a horrible disease that is eating my bones and my lungs and I am dying and I need to be flown to a beach in Germany, it must be Germany, to rest in the shade and to hear German songs. I love you. And now I don't love you. I love you again. Now I don't. I unbutton my jacket and I knot my undershirt so that it sits just below my breasts. I pull the ends of my hair. Doesn't hurt. Doesn't nothing. I walk, a strut, a swoop, a death prance. Birds flying against the wind, but not me. My body home to new lusts. The sun seems dim. My stride is pornographic. My balance is impeccable. I should have a halo, a whip and a tiger. If there were open bottles on the sidewalk I would drink from them. If a man with a cigar walked by me I would finish his cigar in one inhalation and then I would ask him to live with me in a hotel in a language I invented on the spot. Transfixed, he would nod yes. There, we would order food and take showers all day and then finally I would beg him to jump from the window. He would. I would jump after him and land like a cat. He would be dead and, like a cat, I would walk away from him and find someone else to circle.

I climb a hydro pole and I sing 'Angel of the Morning' as loud as I can. A small crowd forms below me. They eat their sandwiches and pick at their nail polish and twist the braids in their hair and they point at me. When I am done, I climb down and I break them with the flint of my eyes. Every look is a match against stone. They will never forget me. Now I know what it is to be you.

Queen Street. Parkdale's jugular. Sausage and scaffolding, dog shit and the dust of construction – the city curdles in a messy inverted maniac love with itself. A current of heat claps against me. I have opened the door to an incinerator and inside it is the sun and it does a great yawn. A comet in a boxcar. I squint. My eyes spot. The tops of the buildings are cut and curled like they are saloons from the days of yore, making Toronto, for a moment, a frontier town, and us, with our packed bags and our business, its new settlers, hurrying to cheat and beg and bleed and peddle and hang our handwritten signs – the paint still wet, and so hot on this day that it will not dry. There is not one cloud in the sky. The road should be dirt. Chickens should be running loose and dizzy.

Not looking ahead of me, but above, seeing my rope tied between clock towers and buildings, spider silk embalming the sky, and I am walking heel-toe, heel-toe, heel-toe, I slam into something. Hard as the hide of a bull. I fall to the pavement. Hit my head. A moment of blackness. The jog of my brain. I look up. The sun, a white-yellow blaze behind him, I cannot make out his face. Only his outline. And it is unruly. An etching from one of Marta's books. The mutineer. Hair in wet tendrils, it drips. He is his own weather system.

'I am so sorry.' The man hoists me up with a kind of jester leap, so strong I slam into him again. 'Sorry.'

I pull my face from his chest. He smells of the lake. The middle of it. Where it is two hundred feet deep, and you might find a piano on the bottom.

'I was looking up,' I say.

'I was looking down. You won't believe the things people lose.'

There is a formality to his way of speaking like he is trying on the words, seeing if they fit. Immaculata told me, overarticulating, 'Children are born with the capacity to speak every language as they adapt to their environment they discard the shapes for syllables and vowels they deem to be unnecessary we should try to adapt Euge we should really try to adapt.' The man forgot to throw away these extra shapes. His mouth is crowded with the sounds of every alphabet. He could pronounce anything.

He is carrying a cooking pot, which hangs from one hand. A grey shoelace pulls his hair back off his face. His eyes troll from the toes of my boots up to the crown of my head and then back down again, pausing at my belly button. He stares at it. Just when I think it is a blue finch and he will stroke it, he leads me to a bench, protectively, as though I am blindfolded. We sit and pull our knees up to our chests. The two of us, beside each other, forgotten accordions, waiting to be opened and played.

'I found a coin once outside a bus station. When I picked it up, I thought, only one thing is this heavy in a hand.' The man's eyes are elfin in shape, tapered at the corners. They are the colour of gun smoke. 'Gold.'

'My sister used to find all kinds of things.' I picture the small, soft bodies of rodents, snakes and bats swirling in jars under her bed, her zigzagged afghan pulled down around them. She lay on her back between them and painted the black slates of her cot into constellations and planets. *To them Euge this is the universe.*

'Are you all right?'

I nod. He beams, making creases of his face.

'You don't have a concussion? I won't have to wake through the night?'

He laughs a molten-core laugh. His laugh is older than he is. When he is finished, he hums a bit.

He has a tuxedo stripe down his black pants. He is wearing tennis shoes. They are also wet. He could tell me that he swam here, with nothing but his cooking pot, and I would believe him. He could tell me that his cooking pot holds the lake, and now, when I look out, all I will see is a piano.

He tilts the pot toward me. It is three inches deep with fresh raspberries. 'Please.'

I put one in my mouth. It is the taste of a lost body part.

'They came early this year. I pick them by the tracks. At the end of Dunn Avenue.' He lifts a finger to his mouth, it is tipped with dirt. 'Don't tell anyone.'

I find myself leaning in toward him. 'I won't.'

His hands and arms are scratched. White shirt rolled up to the elbows, it is spattered red across the shoulders, the shirt of a man shot at while dancing. He had to fight for the raspberries.

'I am making a pie,' he says.

'Our neighbours made a pie until they burned their house down.'

'They probably wanted a fire. Not a pie.'

I see the twins, their skin hardening into scales, how they enacted disaster for their mother's touch. How they stood in front of their oven as it flared into an inferno. How they made themselves stay before it, considering it an unusual flower – one they could not help but pick. What we will do to be touched.

The CN train hurtles across the bridge at Queen and Dufferin, shaking the round-windowed tower of the Gladstone Hotel. A great clang and grunt against the rails. The man covers my ears until it passes. The undersides of his hands are rough. His skin is the colour of chestnuts. Drifter skin. He sleeps beside a camp-fire and when he whistles a horse appears.

I watch him eat a raspberry. If I kissed him, he would bite my bottom lip, my shoulder blade too. Immaculata would call him *lupine*.

He asks me a second time, 'Are you all right?'

I nod.

We stare out at the people tramping the sidewalk. We sit in silence. We have already had every conversation we need to have. We have completed a most exhausting cycle, and we have finally found this bench to rest on together. We could sit here and do nothing but grow old, and one day be declared prehistoric. We could turn each other into icons and then mortals and then icons again. We have already dangled those two words, *love me*, like beads on a fine string. We have already witnessed those beads fall and scatter. We agree that the people rushing by us appear to be prac-ticing war. They are chasing their beads. We're not. We are sitting this war out. We have only just come home.

We finish the raspberries. Our lips are stained red – our mouths new, flamboyant birthmarks. The man's hair is dry. I could not drag my fingers through it. They would never find their way out.

I look into the emptied pot.

'What will you do now?'

'Pick more.'

There is no question of whether I will go with him. We do not run in packs. We keep each other separate, and in so doing, keep ourselves intact. The man walks away, in the direction of where I used to live. Suspenders hang from the back of his pants. His body is limber and supple, a slipknot. He could outwit chains and handcuffs. Exit an apiary without being stung. He could have a tortoise on a leash, a gramophone on his shoulder.

'Bye,' I say.

'You're a slim bit of flint.'

His words bound in my head, bulky and flourishing. His accent is placeless. Mink would try to imitate it, but she would never quite get it.

'Is English your first language?' I call after him. He stops and gazes back at me. If his pockets were full, people might accuse him of stealing. He seems to sit on both sides of the law.

'I don't have a first language.' And with that, the man vanishes into the fold.

From our collision, raspberries blot the sidewalk red. They appear like markings at the beginning of a trail. The man's front teeth were capped. And his words in my ear were the snaps and hollers of a dream being remembered.

I will wait for Finbar's response. He is the clue you left for me, the only one. And so, patient as a huntress crouched on a platform high in a tree, I will wait for it. If he is prompt, which I think he will be, given the brightness of the number eighteen, how it flickers, it should take two days. And with his letter, I will hope that, in accordance with some decent frontier-town barter, he will include a map, and that once I follow the map, there you will be, cigarette between your teeth, smoke rising in powdered wigs and signatures. You will tell me you wished you could give me a world that was only beautiful but that this is impossible. And then, your face a downpour of tears, you will drive it through the nearest pane of glass to give yourself a new scar, your most formidable yet, as apology.

{ POSTCARD FROM OUTER SPACE }

eugeniamydarlin',

distance nothing but a line between us.
one we will walk.

s

The morning after Mink comes home from Sudbury (eye roll) smelling of menthol, you find Urszula Minor dead in the backyard. You had seven stray cats: Sirloin, Madame Balcony, the Naturalist, Peter Frampton, Rococo and Mighty Digger. But Urszula — elegant, minuscule, tailless — was your favourite. You would bring her a bowl of food every night balanced in your filthy shoemaker hands. While she ate, your boot would circle the dirt around her, trenching a moat. You wanted her to live with us, to perch on your shoulders while you painted, to curl up at the end of your bed. But Mink would *have none of it*. Turning the vacuum cleaner off with the kind of kick that starts a motorcycle, she said, *Urszula is probably drowning in fleas*. She wasn't then. But she sure is now.

Urszula's body is mangled and mud-glazed. She lies stiff under the apple tree. A bowl from the wedding-china cabinet sits beside her, licked clean. You swear that she was poisoned. You pull her to you, crumple over like a page on fire, and you yell her name. *Ula*. You called her *Ula* for short. *Ula. Ula*. You shout it over and over again. *Ula*. A curse that has filled you up. *Ula. Ula. Ula*. You break through the back door. Blood freckles your hands and neck, thick splinters to your hair. You clear off the kitchen table and you lay her down. Immaculata broods beside you, fitful and sparring, a body trapped in a burlap sack. Mink's brow knits. She is searching for an answer.

I want to be the body on the table. I want to be the name that has taken you. I want to be your curse. Immaculata, suddenly very calm, pulls you away from Urszula and intones, 'She's gone Sheb she's gone.' You glower and then all the muscles in your face die. You turn to me. Your eye could tumble out.

You retreat to your bedroom and stay there for three days, hitting your soft head against the wall.

Urszula is the first thing I have ever seen that is dead. Aside from Immaculata's clippings in the folder labelled DEATH and the photograph of Lenin in his coffin, which she keeps, like a portrait of the Queen, above her bed. 'I bet the mourners did not know that his mouth is sewn shut true that's what the embalmers did sewed your mouth shut true sick but neat whoa,' Immaculata told me and then quickly sutured her mouth before pinning the photograph there below her reading light.

'Death makes you available for anything'

'Death can make you carry a placard for something you do not believe in.'

'Death can make you wear an argyle suit.'

I study the photograph. Death is being trapped in a strange mould while others stand above you, wondering what they will look like dead. Wondering if they too will look glue-coloured. Wondering when.

Immaculata is an expert in life expectancies. While she deftly alternates Urszula's body between the freezer and the oven – preserving her until you are ready to bury her – she determines that, 'By the looks of it, Urszula Minor is close to twenty years old this is plenty of life for a cat Euge should I tell him cause of death was nature?'

'No.' You prefer to be a habitation for injury. You prefer the sting complete.

Immaculata smooths Urszula's coat. Mink is too engrossed doing an inventory of the wedding china to notice that she has snuck her silver-handled hairbrush to do the job.

I sit in the hallway outside your bedroom, waiting to be admitted entry. The house is so quiet without your threats to impale yourself, to throw yourself on a bed of cacti, to shoot yourself with Mink's prop gun, without your stomping and your shouts, your claps, your clumsiness – things dropped and broken – your orders to clamour around the radio, tears falling in wet strands from your eyes, necklaces shining more brightly than anything else. Without your muddy footprints over the vacuumed strips of the carpet left there like a diagram for a dance student to step into.

You moan to yourself to drown out the noise of the sun. *Ula. Ula. Ula.* You say it over and over again. Until the word is just vowels. Limp darts to the light. The shadows grow longer. Afternoon. You step to the window and pull back the curtain, a sniper. Everyone appears to you as Urszula Minor's murderer. The postman. Clotilda and Yufeng with their grocery bags of bread and peanuts. Clotilda's mute son polishing his silver car. Even Tuberculosis Flo with her hair band and pigtails. Even Elsie. Even Mink.

Children gather to play hopscotch in front of our house. They draw white lines on the sidewalk. You lean your head out the window and you say in a whisper-staccato, the sound of blades, smoke coming out of your mouth, *scat scat scat.* And, frightened, they do. They split apart in a run, their schoolbags falling from their shoulders, laces coming undone. They start to spread rumours about our house. A madman lives there. He is tower-tall and he never washes and he never sleeps and his wife is a witch and his daughters are pale ghosts, and if they speak to you, run, it's a trap, because if you answer, your mouth will be sewn shut. Now when they walk by, the children, without a glance our way, cross the street. The chalk clutched in their small hands, to you, the wretched vial.

When you do finally emerge, the groan of your dresser pushed aside and the door creaked open three inches, you squint at the hallway light. A slice of your face and, behind you, your room is a darkened theatre. You don't even know who I am. 'I won't paint anymore,' you murmur. And with that, my heart does a kind of lurch and makes the low screech of a tanker running up against rock.

'Just let me keep Eugenia.' You are begging.

'But I'm here.'

You beg until you go hoarse.

'But I'm here.'

An air howl. And then, your mouth still moving, you close the door. The skid of your dresser scratching the bedroom floor.

{POSTCARD FROM OUTER SPACE}

e(quatorial). e(cstatic). e(xcelsis deo). e(ugenia).

contrary to fairy tales, stars don't shine.
they are so old that they are dead.
this makes space the perfect hideout.

invitation.

still no neighbours. skin to the wind.

s

Now to find a place to rest my head on this bag of onions and money before I stalk our former home and the postman who, bandy in his postman shorts, smells of broth. I head east along Queen Street, toward the ferry docks, toward the lake, feet sure as any migratory instinct.

'Those are some boots, mama.' A man in a leather hat with skin that matches tosses this out to me, tipping his brim, junk shop behind him, birdcages and suitcases making fragile towers. His face is a plate that has been shot in the air. 'I'd follow you to the grave, I would.' This time he sounds serious. A filthy swallow dips his beak into the last shrinking puddle below him and, together, the man and his bird usher in my age, my new age, the age of eighteen. Its thirst.

I feel as if I have been away. As if I've stood at the bottom of an ocean floor. Walked through snow thick as a blindfold. Been dragged behind a horse, pine gum in my hair. And now, returned, I have misplaced some things and forfeited others. In their absence, new things have chuted in to claim their place. They are just slightly harder to the touch, bones that much more fused. I stop in front of the beautician's window to inventory, not sure what form they'll take, these souvenirs. I could have a tricycle in my pocket. I could be covered in moon dust. I could have gloom for eyes. I could be cured with salt.

Mink takes me here the day of my ninth birthday. The beautician is blind. Her pupils pale and aimless. Her own hairdo a bit crooked, a slightly disappointing cake. But no one would ever tell her. Not because of her blindness but because she does not lend herself to other people's opinions. This is what I like about her most. This is why I remember her and her beclouded eyes. She smells of cupcakes and talcum powder. When Mink apologizes for me having *ants in my pants*, the beautician says that she understands the restlessness of children. She has five children of her own — all named for countries she has never been to and knows she will never see. *Chortle, chortle*, she laughs and clutches her chest. I realize that she smells of her children, that she just cannot get enough of touching them. Driving home, Mink says, 'With those names, her kids'll be exotic dancers.' Mink laughs hard. It is the sound of a turbine. She steams the front window. In the mist, I write EUGENIA. I imagine it to be the name of a country.

Luxembourg. Côte d'Ivoire. Tuvalu. Belarus. Yemen. Eugenia.

'Are you issuing passports for Eugenia?' Mink asks, looking at me, my shellacked up-do. Her eyes flitting back and forth across my face, she is reading the same urgent signal again and again.

'Would you like one?'

'Yes.'

And then we grow quiet; we are the first to round a corner and stumble upon a hidden dominion, fog to our waists, a thatch of forest beyond.

Today, a sign on the door in a child's handwriting reads CLOSED DUE TO FAMILY EMERGENCY. I cup my hands and peer in the window. Hair lies unswept on the floor. Octopi. Dust has gathered on the leather chairs and the kits of press-on nails and nail polish. Dust has made all the wigs grey.

I take in my reflection. My face is not pure and beautiful. Not nearly as successful a configuration as Mink's or

– 148 –

Immaculata's. The features are too exaggerated, a collage by an impatient child. But I do belong in it. It is mine, this face that could almost be yours. I move in closer. Touch the glass. I miss you. My pupils are a translucent green. Seaweed at the surface of the water, the sun pulsing, blowing them out. My pupils are yours. You should be beside me rolling an apple through your dirt-coloured teeth, sucking on its seeds, spitting them out and turning the city wild with trees.

I reach into my pant pocket to retrieve what I managed to sneak out under Immaculata's watchful gaze: the box of *REDBIRD* matches. *Best to go into the woods alone, Eugenius, then you'll find out for yourself.* And a black-and-white photograph of you. I took it on our camping trip to Darlington. It is the only one I have. Rain is skidded across your face. Blackflies too. A cigarette dangles from your mouth, you are mid-story. I pin the photograph to my back. Surely someone will recognize you. Sheb Wooly Ledoux. Surely you were that well-known. I pin the photograph to my back. Just in case I cannot find what I am looking for.

{ POSTCARD FROM OUTER SPACE }

from the last whole earth catalog,
the 'treaty for outer space'
prepared in geneva 1966
includes this clause,
senate approved 88 to 0:
if an astronaut lands on another country's soil he must be
returned safely, promptly and unconditionally.

A heap of wedding dresses lies on the stairs of the Salvation Army, exhausted swans. Washed up in them, sirens spit from sea froth, is a pair of drunks, their hair long and white, sneakers falling off, jeans too. Sherry nocturnes lift from their skin, their faces puffed with sleep. Noses bulbous, eyes shut like those of fresh babies, the men hold hands. Their breath skims the surface, short and quivering. Under the midday sun, they are the red of boxing gloves, then the brown of spittoon, then the black of asphalt. They are birthday candles, drooping and sloping wax, and they are burning up here.

In them, I see Finbar. His wooden teeth, his wandering eyes, the silvery disks that traverse them. At a round eighty years old, a death ripeness warms over him. It walks between his rooms. Curling a fingertip here. Whitening a hair there. Eating a vertebra. All of it the crook and hue of ash. But the desertion he hates to name is this one: his senses are going. His mouth is so bland now, given what it once was, pressed up against the hipbones of women, searching their crevices, their earlobes, his tongue in the small of a back reading the imprint of a button – knowing where it was made and from what wood, what shell. He could, at one time, smell a woman in an airplane flying overhead; the sky itself had turned to steeple – a steeple of rose blossoms, juniper and anise, and below it, he worshipped. Swaying on his property, grass to his waist, he nosed that roof of woman, and he waved with two hands, hungry, so hungry, save me, save me from this body, so sick with lament.

Worse, though, is his mind. What was once a steel trap for the birthdates of warriors, the Latin etymology of names and the sequence of Baudelaire's *Les Fleurs du mal* is failing. He was a raconteur of delirious proportions and, everyone agreed, the performer of the best party tricks. He could loosen a pair of silk stockings from across a room. By the time he got home, his pockets would be spilling with them. Shed snakeskins. He would press them to his nose and guess the wearers' addresses correctly. He could seduce anyone's wife. Within twelve words, she would be climbing up on a table and loosening a hook from an eye. Within twenty, his son-of-a-farmer hands steadying her ankles, she would be stepping out of her petticoats. He could strip a duchess and be given her crown while she was being sworn in. He could make a woman come or cry, depending on his whim. He could ruin your life in a morning if he felt so inclined. But now the small has become too big, the big too small. When Finbar looks for something, it sneaks out of view never to return, his mind migratory as driftwood. He is losing operas to breadcrumbs.

After his beloved fell, Finbar never walked the rope again. He was forty-five years old – probably your age now. He retreated to the woods, his location unspecified, but early speculation pegged it to be near the Alaskan border, in the dredges of an abandoned mining camp, a radius of eighty miles uninhabited around him, to feed on his grief. Despite his isolation, and that Cubist face, Finbar had visitors. It was said that any girl who walked past his gates would be undone – the tinker's daughter, the tailor's, the chief's – and they would all re-emerge with child. Finbar planted his seed and his seed spread, giving his house the provocative moniker Orphan Stadium. He was an illusionist, nowhere and everywhere at once.

When Finbar grew bored of the girls, their bodies lustreless in the pitch of morning, he kicked them out of Orphan Stadium and they hanged themselves from the willow trees that surrounded the fiery yawn of his home. Not suicides but graduated lovers. Fallen daughters, they suspended themselves in lighted husks, iridescent pods. Promises. Offerings. Fireflies in cases, waiting to be cracked open again, by him. Illustrious I. I., carnivorous I. I., natural disaster, demigod and host to a kingly erection that was rumoured to last for entire days. He was inexhaustible. The girls would show him their breasts when he took out the garbage. If he took out the garbage.

Recalling your voice now, deep like it is made of dirt and syrup and you have to summon it up from your toenails all the way to your throat, I wonder, is Finbar, eighty years old, asleep in a pile of dead women's dresses, still a spell? And if so, am I, in preparing to meet him, just an egg waiting to be smashed?

When you introduced me to Finbar, and you dipped your fingers, caked, cracked and stained mustard-seed yellow, into balsam wax, making a ruler out of your moustache in the style of his, I did not tell you that I beat you to him. For this past year, when you locked yourself away for days at a time, to claw the dark, to fall into your mattress, the feathers and cotton coagulating in parts, cutting into you, *cut me, this bitter rind, taking root*, his *Unofficial Autobiography* became the one book that I could recite by rote. It was not the titillating details – the grocer's daughter, the piano tuner's, the auctioneer's (though these were an education unto themselves) – but his training that captured me, and that, in a way, made me his own. You were not the only one to leaf through the book like you had discovered your family album.

What you saw as miracles — balls caught in the crook of my neck, roofs walked, chairs tipped and climbed, a handstand on a crane — you did not know were the result of hours spent stretching and lifting and making myself strong, a perfectly stacked axis, all in the method of Finbar, all in the anticipation that one day I too would step onto the wire.

four

I reach Ward's Island just as night falls – netting over a mourner's eyes. From here, Toronto is a vision of the future. Bright and tall, the buildings big as the first computers. Sheet lightning pitchforks the sky. Whenever we saw lightning, Immaculata would recite a passage from *A Handbook of Renaissance Meteorology*. She would address that effusion of light, describing it to itself, intimating it did not understand its power, 'This burns a man inward and consumes the body to ashes without harming the garments it stays the youngling in the womb without harm to the mother it consumes money the purses remaining whole.' When you vanished, this is what I feared I would find: your suit laid out, ashen and rumpled on the floor of your studio, the effigy of a disintegrated man. I could not help but feel that you were the conduit for a phenomenon, a punishing force I could not begin to give words to.

Your hands would always shake, but the moment your brush touched the canvas, they were still. Painting, you finally left the atmosphere. Your paintings were you. Melancholic voluptuaries, they were paintings your collectors would kill to bed, to love, to know. Paintings they could never tire of but would instead tire of them. You did them in one sitting, convinced that *people need to experience the making of the thing*. Always working in the same method – from the top left corner down. Your subjects with their pipes, their mutts, their mandolins, lay naked and corpulent, legs spread wide. Others were bony, their eyes closed, your sink in the corner, its pipes exposed. One woman slept beside her thin dog. You called the woman Cupid. She slept for three days. You hated when people posed. Somnolent Cupid and her dog, the hull of her ribs, the pink-blue ribbon of his tongue, were perfect.

You layered the paint so thickly your paintings would never completely dry. Leaning in, too close, viewers were immediately clowns, the ends of their noses turned red, yellow, grey. They wanted to creep into your paintings. To live them. To be their slashes and gouges. They did not know the danger of their wish. That you had barely come through their making, and that if you were anywhere but that magnificent hall, rushed by admirers, their stained noses a black comedy, you would collapse and tell me that the sea level was rising, and soon it would reach your bed.

Lake churning white beneath, the islanders descend the ferry by bicycle. They pull carts behind them filled with groceries and children and various supplies: wood, soil, plants. Blackbirds hop around them, music notes that have jumped from a page. One boy eats ice cream from a carton with a toothbrush. He has a friar's haircut and a squiggle for a mouth. A girl fans a fly from her arm. Her eyes are a washed-out brown, as if, in a low mood, she added too much water to them. The islanders' skin is blushed, radishes. They do not lock their doors. They do not have basements. They have ninety-nine-year leases. They are a different kind of settler. A blackbird lands on my head, its sure scrawl against my scalp. Welcome. *Bird's nest.* Mink would laugh.

Toronto Island is a sandspit. From above, it appears as a collection of rocks smoothed flat for luck by a nervous hand. Marbled by water, it is composed of fourteen islands in total, the archipelago coming together in a thick hook shape at its western end. The island was formed over the course of 10,000 years. After the Scarborough Bluffs were bullied into being by the last ice age, Toronto deaf under a kilometre of ice, the bluffs were carried by wind and currents to form a peninsula. The night of April 14, 1858, a storm broke the peninsula's neck, separating it from Toronto for good and founding the island. It was, like so many things, born out of a natural and lengthy violence.

The small cottages that dot Ward's and Algonquin islands could be wrapped in wool, and, smoke piping through their chimneys, converted into warm, square kettles. Trails are worn between them. Their light is Marta's light, golden and trembling. Maybe she is here. Lit matches in her hands, lending halos to her wrists, skimming over dog bones and the discarded lines of poems. Maybe this is the afterlife and the afterlife is incandescence, and I will spend the next two days playing dead.

The islanders ride past me, their loads shuddering over the wooden slats as they climb the bridge to their cottages. They bid each other goodnight. I wish for them to stop. To pluck me up and to drop me into their carts, to invite me in and swing their arms around me like ivy. But they fly by in a broad front, determined to return to their homes, far away from that vision of the future.

It is so quiet here without the noise of the city – and without you, your dissertations, renunciations, your strivings, disappointments, your cries in the night, your telephone calls to strangers. You would dial *operator*, offer up a city, *say Toledo*, and you would guess a last name, and then you would be connected, *hello Toledo!* and you would converse with Toledo about their favourite food, favourite pastimes, favourite music. *Favourites! Portal into a stranger!* And to everything, you would say, *Me too!* It was so easy for you to slip, a cat smoothing himself under a fence, into another person's heart. You would never call again, even though you would repeat their number back to them, slowly, deliberately, as if you were making a note of it on your forearm. But it was just an accident in the first place, one you could never recover. Plus, there were so many other strangers. So many other cities. *Say Calcutta. Say Huntsville. Say Buenos Aires.* So many other fences to get under.

Lake Shore Avenue cuts through the island, from its eastern to its western point. I follow it. My boots are the only percussion against the pavement. Otherwise, it is completely abandoned. No trucks. No bicycles. No geese. Its surroundings too. Dirt and scrub and sky. A scrupulous minimalism. I am a fleck between civilizations. Shot from a cannon, wandering a land that I do not know. I pass the fire station, the fountain, the public washrooms and the lockers checked orange and blue. I can smell the charcoal and the meat from the day's picnics. A sunbather's blanket lies crinkled in the sand. A ball. A harmonica. A shoe sideways in the grass. Did everyone have to tidy all at once and leave in a hurry? Was there a great rush, and they had to run, dropping their things and only half-dressed? Or maybe everyone is hiding. In the fountain. Behind that poplar. Under that table. Maybe they saw me coming and this emptiness is a game. I look down. A mound of apple cores.

Past the filtration plant, and past the lighthouse, all the props of human living are suddenly gone. I could sleep here, hidden and safe beneath the brambles, but I don't. I go on – pulled by a fishing wire looped around my waist, one hand, rough and sure, a black thumbnail, winding it on the other end. If someone did come upon me, my searching face, they would guess *amnesiac* and then they would spin me around and pronounce,

Look, her only clue, about the photograph pinned to my back. Not knowing what else to do, not knowing you, they would send me on my way.

I wade deeper into the dark. It coats my skin and begins to claim me as its own. The air is cooler here, fever-wet. I know that there is a lagoon nearby; I can smell the tall grasses, the mulch at the surface of the water. The lake is on my left. It laps the shore, tired. Its edge cluttered with the refuse of the day. At this end of the island, near Hanlan's Point, there used to be homes. Two hundred of them. A baseball diamond. A fairground. A dancehall. A theatre. Three hotels. I hear the flounce of a long skirt brush through the grass. The breath of a boy running through laundry lines to the carnival, coins skipping in his pockets. A hammer slung from a leather belt. An enamelled dish dropped on a stair. A girl peeling cucumbers for a sandwich. For a moment I can see all of them, their shadows bristling and hungry. And then, with a snarl, they are gone. This night: a black that is vacancy. The houses were bulldozed. The only evidence that anyone ever lived here at all is the walls built at the shore to battle the strength of the lake, which always threatened to drown them. Now some plastic bags are caught in the branches. They inflate with the wind like store-bought ghosts. The horn of the last ferry sounds. Everything stops just for that moment to listen.

I think about the girl with the rope. *Always in the same untravelled clearing in the woods, between the jackfruit and the betel nut, bamboo creepers, the jamun and the mango.* When the flood comes to wipe out her village, she talks to her rope and it rises while she stands on it, lifting her to safety. Below, cats wrap themselves around their owners' sandals, scamper up legs, sit on shoulders and then vault to higher ground. Bats come out like kites. Rats and dogs start to claw up chimneys, the sides of buildings, nearby hills. 'Watch the animals,' you said to me, 'always watch the animals.' The village is the sound of scurrying. No shouts, no hollers yet, only the sprint of animal paws. And then suddenly a groan, and the mud-brown water barrels down on them, rounding up umbrellas and wedding gowns, gulping trucks and bodies and boats. A boy rides the current on a bare mattress. He screams and it sounds almost like exultation. And then everything disappears. The earth is coated anew. It is a planet for the girl to discover first.

The wind picks up again, and I have the sensation that I am being watched. Heartbeat-footsteps-heartbeat-footsteps heartbeat-footsteps. My mind is mice scrambling across floorboards. *Best to go into the woods alone, Eugenius, then you'll find out for yourself.* I light a match. The wind so strong now everything is bantamweight; the match is blown out. I stretch my arms in front of me, a sleepwalker miles from home, groping the dark, fingers reading it because my eyes cannot. This is the Great Unknown. I inch along the road, night tying my ankles tight together. Something waits for me here, and I have yet to bump up against it.

'Hello.'

Is it a string of children holding hands, so still they were cut from paper? Is it two black storks stumbling and pirouetting? Is it a crater? An open mouth? Your hundred daughters? Dressed in suits, hair cut in slices? A hunched figure in the ditch. Is it you? Holding your breath. Boo. I blink, lids hard shutters, but nothing will clear.

A rustle in the woods. The snap of a twig. I stop. Clocking. 'Sheb?'

The trees stretch out in a conspiracy-whisper around me. In them, movement. Unmistakable. Blood thumps in my ears. My heart pounds, a fist against a coffin, so loud that if someone called out to me, I would not hear them. I make out a man. Your dimensions. He moves so quickly in the woods that he is a forest fire leaping a highway and becoming two fires.

'Sheb.'

I chase you. The branches are crabs, curled and thick lines, they toss me, biting through my suit. You wanted to die a hero's death, you told me. You wanted to be gored by a bull. 'What an epitaph, my darlin', to have a set of horns through your rib cage,' you would say, 'what an epitaph.' This is how I feel as I fight my way toward you: horns through my rib cage.

But there is nothing there – only the sound of your voice in my head, *Stunt*, a vapour, a velvet, a million birds I cannot name. I could vanish here. My onions, my withering, browning, hollowed shrine hanging above me. Or I could walk into the water, an inky twin to the night, and let it steal me away. No. I smooth my suit down and I walk back to the road. I am determined to return to my home.

'He says he's not painting anymore.' Mink is on the recliner in the living room reading the *World Weekly News*, her hair singing under the light. On the cover, a boy in a diaper is waving. The caption reads: Boy Freeze Dried By Parents. Mink drops it, stands and shakes out her legs. Brow unknit, she heads to your studio so quickly that she makes the sound of an arrow shot to the wind.

You have left the door unlocked. 'Hm.' Mink walks in. Partly finished canvases are propped up against the walls, work lights on, photographs fingered on the edges, half-broken stereos and eight-track players below, garbage that you combed the streets for (*Thursday night is garbage night!*) and came close to repairing, the projector and the sheet that shone our movies. Boxes are piled high and dusted over. An ancient civilization to be excavated and reassembled. Gallery openings, invitations, packs of matches, yellowed receipts from the Waverley Hotel and the Spadina Hotel for Men, train tickets, newspaper clippings and unfilled prescriptions – all of which I would handle like thousand-year-old tools.

I was the one you let purr into the studio. I was the one who named your paintings. Your last opening: I was the one grinning beside you, my flight pattern an imitation of yours, my Lilliputian body. Every time you had to shake a hand, you let go of mine. Returned quickly to it. Your impossibly long stride through the gallery, your gait one that I could swing between, the slap of your boots on the marble, musk in the air having returned from the other side and translated it for us. Your paintings were divine stunts. Shake my hand. Touch me. I rode on your shoulders, the two of us forming the grand back of an elephant, an epic sauntering through the crowd. Everyone parted for us. Sometimes you lifted me in the air with one hand. I would spread my arms, born from your palm, and people would look on, the innate surprise of seeing a Siamese creature.

Your paintings were the bison and pregnant mares of cave drawings to me. Carved into limestone, scattering under the light, they were your effort to make a record of the human experience in all of its relentless motion. They were your attempt to be still. Alongside your collection of birth announcements, the story of our hunt was up to you.

Mink moves in the swift unblinking manner of nurses, impressively looping thick rope around your half-finished canvases, your sketchbooks and your brushes. Now deemed useless materials. Now corralled. She bags your tubes of paint, palettes, books, your trinkets, your photographs, ticket stubs, scraps and articles. The knife, the rope and the bags were in her black cardigan pocket, cashmere. Did she know that you would come to this decision? Was she just biding her time until you made your announcement? She does not seem disturbed by it. It is as though all of your friends have died and Mink does not see this as loss — only that with their deaths, you have been returned to her, and that all of the time you might have spent with them is now free to be spent with her — and she will win you and charm you and heal you so that you forget all about death, you forget all about the others. She will wipe you clean.

She brings out the toothbrush for the second time. And then she hauls everything out to the curb. It makes a tidy heap.

No one touches it. It reads too much like a hex. Your last portrait sits on top. A left eye, floating.

When the garbagemen come in the dawn in their orange suits and their safety gloves, you do not watch them make away with your work. But Mink, a fanatic for the solid line of completion, does. She stands by the window, and when they drive away, she makes a sound, a tickle in her throat. The only thing left, at my insistence: the birth announcements. Laid out like the beginnings of a city.

In the backyard, below the apple tree, a mound at her feet, shovel propped against her side, hands raw from digging, Immaculata holds Urszula aloft and calls to me, 'Eugenia she is ready to be buried now or else!' The cat is a mascot for herself – both of them resplendent in their white beaded headbands, their smoothed coats.

I bolt from the house, a drunk with a destination, white sunglasses frames crooked on my face. I run up the street, past the church, past Leopold of the Onions, his finger up, 'Wait,' past the prostitutes, 'Honeychild,' 'Sugarlumps,' 'Sister Pain,' and past the mission. The sky is the blade of an axe, and below it the city dwellers are hurried and desperate, just short of clawing each other. I weave between them and stop in front of the library, hands clapped over my ears. Parkdale's shipwrecked drape the stairs. I step over the men, pickled, parka-ed and tossing prayer and insult to the wind.

I open the door. Quiet as a capsule. The librarian looks up at me, her head a bird-twitch. I bird twitch back and wander the stacks. It has been three days since you locked yourself in your bedroom. Even when you are at your most unreachable, there is always a sliver, a hole that only I can crawl through. Threading a needle. But not this time. I need another world, one that will force me to forget the red swell of your eyes, the soundless marathon of your mouth, your vow to stop painting. I find the heaviest book in the place and pull it down. It is a cannonball in my hands.

Black and leather-bound. The lettering, gold and ornate. Trilled at the edges.

I. I. Finbar Me the Three,
Handsome Funambulist and Colossal Menagerie:
An Unofficial Autobiography

On the back cover: 'The trick is to have a stunt that no one else can perform.' The words stop me dead.

The book smells of mould and mildew; it has just been brought up from a basement and placed here by a drowned woman with palm leaves for hands and snails for eyes. I hear her wet call. The centre of it falls open. Photographs. Glossy and dated long before I was born.

1914. Finbar's first walk. In the posters around Avening, Ontario, a farming town northwest of the city, he billed himself Boy Wonder. Not yet thirteen years old, he stands on the wire, arms outstretched, a scarecrow thirty feet above a field of corn. A small crowd is gathered below him. Stalks to their chests. Arms crossed over, they are arguing against the very thing they are seeing. The rest of his hometown are in their shops and kitchens staring at their radios. In petrified silence, they listen to the first moments of the War to End All Wars. The Russians are mobilizing. The townspeople's faces fall. But Finbar, triumphant, does not.

1920. Here is Finbar, now 'I. I. Finbar Me the Three,' a young man of nineteen in striped tights and leather shoes. Pitchforks, scalpels, razors and butcher knives spike the ground silver. He walks above them, blindfolded. 'Inexhaustible!' Finbar balances on one foot, a line of flame leaping below him. And then, most stunning, is Finbar's first ascension, 160 feet above the whirlpools of Niagara Falls. The surface is a scramble of hard waves. It is the white of molars, stealing itself away and then feeding itself back into being. Finbar walks in a sack. And then he does somersaults on stilts, and then he hangs from his bare feet, a prehistoric bird.

I enter the photograph; the division of time and place dissolves. It is as if Finbar has already met Death and so Death does not hover about him. Finbar, in his tights and his leather shoes, crossed a room, pulled back a chair and sat at Death's oak table. He pinched the ends of his moustache smooth and he bargained. He bought time. With what, I wonder. What did he have to give away to do this? The shoreline is thick with people. I hold my breath, body pressed between them, and there I am taught for the first time: possibility.

'Please refrain from speaking in the library.' The librarian is beside me. So close, she fogs my face. She grew up in a farmhouse, an only child, looking out at a river, with her aunt's appendix in a jar on a shelf in her bedroom. 'You are talking to yourself.'

'Oh?'

She lifts a finger to her lips. 'Sh.'

I nod. Her hands are chapped and packing-plant-clean, nails painted black with press-on moons and stars. The 'sh' one is taped.

'I understand exuberance.' She is small, my height, with a soft stomach. You could punch it down like dough and feel her spine there at the bottom, a ring recovered from a lake. She crosses her arms, reading my mind.

'I'm sorry,' I say, cancelling the thought.

'It's all right.' She studies my face. 'Do your parents take care of you?'

We speak to each other in low tones, like we are an endangered species and do not want to be found out. We twitch and then she returns to her desk.

In the photographs, dated from the mid-forties to the mid-sixties, Finbar is always a figure in the distance, his face inscrutable —

a lantern in a snowstorm. I see that he is strong and broad. True to his farm stock. He could clear an entire field of stones and build a fence with them in an afternoon, fell a tree and carry it out of the forest on one shoulder. I see that he walked the beams of his barn while his family slept, swallows spiralling into a smoke signal through a hole in the roof. I see that he used sheep and then horses and then steers for weights, having hypnotized the animals with whispers into their keen ears. In the dark, he lifted them, steam coming out of their nostrils, their brains on fire. His chest always bare — I can imagine his vanity.

When I turn the page, I see his face for the first time. It is grotesque. As if he survived a great storm, but his features, after being bashed by the air, were not returned properly to their places. He was never reformed. His cheeks hang slack in pouches from bones that look stolen from a strongman's thigh. His jaw is puffed wide and then tapers too long near his clavicle. His lips and nose are purpling fruit. And, skull mushrooming above and below them, Finbar's eyes appear to be two black points. Period. In them, there is only one thing: the power of a man who gets his own way. His hair is thick and blond. It hangs down to his shoulders. And his moustache, the only fine line. When Finbar looked in the mirror, wax on his fingertips, this is where he focused his attentions. Upon sight of him, Mink would have stifled a laugh and then she would have grown very quiet and stared. You would beg to paint his portrait. And then you would wish that his face, that squall, were your own.

The second-last photograph is of Finbar standing beside a woman, pale and long as an icicle. Freezing or melting, one can never be sure. I can see that, in her, Finbar finally found someone more powerful than himself. Finbar's arm clasped around her waist is a python. If it were not there, she would be kicking up dirt. The woman is not exquisite, but if she were in a crowded room, she would be the only one you would want to look at. Her eyes: too close together and ringed with coal. Her nose: Roman. Her cheekbones: too high into her temples. Torso too short, legs too long, breasts heaving and full on such a thin frame. With these proportions, her clothes never completely fit. It is like she is always soaking wet, having just emerged from a lake no one else can find.

In this photograph, the woman's dress rides too high on her thigh, black garter peeking out, straps falling down her arms. She is not trying to provoke. Rather, she does not abide by the rules of civility. And every night she slips away and sleeps beside a fire, and wakes in the morning, a fox covered in soot, only to become a woman again. She has the kind of wildness that everyone else trades in too early.

She did not pose for this photograph. She did not sink into the arms of her beloved. No, she challenged the photographer, his request to be still. Please. By the time he got his shot, she was the only subject he ever wanted. Chin thrust in the air, a slender cigarette in one corner of her mouth, and with its smoke she obscures Finbar, his deranged face. Her eyes catch something and she smiles at it, just outside the frame — always just outside the frame.

The woman is referred to only as Finbar's Queen. The last photograph is her tombstone. Untended. 1918–1945. She was twenty-seven years old when she died. After that day, Finbar disappeared from view. He never walked the rope again. Now I know what he bargained when he sat down at the oak table with Death.

I walk home from the library. My steps slow and small, a slight bend at the waist, conjuring a balancing pole there that intersects me. Twilight descends. And with it, so do you.

Your hair is combed like a jailbird just released. Your winter coat is off. Your suit is pressed and free of lint and dandruff. Your cowboy boots are polished. You have shaved your beard. Upon sight of me, you hear an entire symphony in your head and you scoop me up in your arms and you dip me and we dance in great lunges and spins. Over the horn section, you shout, 'Where have you been?'

'Walking.'

'Liar.'

'At the library.'

'Doing what?'

'Reading.'

'About what?'

'Possibility.'

'The possibility of a house other than your house? The possibility of a father other than me?' The symphony ends and you fill the silence with fury.

'No.'

'Don't leave me again.'

'I won't.'

'Promise.'

'I promise.'

'Promise.'

'I just did,' I say, looking around, meeting the eyes on us, 'What?' making them slink into the next fight.

Later that night, you take me to Our Spot by the Lake and you say, settling into the sand, 'One day, my darlin', I will take you to the place where I was born. North. It is a pocked landscape, the flesh of a grapefruit, all horizon, an Arctic desert, an uninterrupted curve.' You jump to standing and, in your boots, you are a slow-motion zero-gravity prowl. 'Everyone bounds a foot and a half off the ground.'

You lift your feet in an astronaut purr, 250,000 miles from the earth, until I ask, 'What about Mink? Will she come too?'

'She wouldn't want to, my darlin'.'

'And Immaculata?'

'She wouldn't either.'

'Did you tell them you're going to take me?'

'No.'

'Will you?'

And then, not answering, you go on, loose as a marionette, tapping your feet and winging your arms, performing your dance again in miniature. 'You can trick yourself that you live in space in the north. It's a twin to the moon, Eugenius. It's where the astronauts train for their missions.' And then you stop. 'What, what are you looking at?' When my eyes should be on you, in your silver suit and matching helmet, defying gravity, a million miles of deep blue around you, they are, for the first time, just outside the frame. Caught on Finbar and his wild Queen, who, together, curl up in me. A secret, they thrive.

For months thereafter, the phone bleats and bleats, the hushed voices of your art dealers and your patrons bent like canes over your casket. They beseech you, but you cannot be reasoned with. After a long silence, you say, 'Yes, I am here. Yes, I am listening. I have not stopped painting because I am depressed.' And then, cradling the receiver, you pull down the portraits that remain on our walls. 'It is the looking I cannot do. I cannot stand to look anymore.' You hang up, pacing our floor now covered in faces, and you mutter, 'Somewhere there is an island full of these things.' Clockwise. When you pace, you pace only clockwise.

Even though there is nothing in there but the birth announcements, you still spend your days in the studio with the door locked. Do you go through them, discovering again and again that you have the birth announcement of everyone in the world but you? Or have you dug a hole in the floor? Do you follow a slender tunnel every day out to a place built of logs on the fast water where the air is always wet? Dressing and undressing, dressing and undressing. Or drills. Dropping to the ground. Pretending disaster. Or sleeping. But you rarely sleep. There is too much to discuss, to read, to taste, to invent, to rage against, to fall in love with. I press a glass to the door, my ear against it. There is no sound. You are not learning how to play a new instrument or how to speak a new language. You are not tumbling. You do not even cough. Or light a match. You do not shuffle your feet. And you do not speak — which makes me wonder if you are even there, so accustomed am I to your fit of words. *I am copyrighting our land! I am unplugging everything! I am reminding myself of my hunter-gatherer instinct in the urban colossus! I am making a saddle in the tradition of the Sioux!* No. Every night, you return to us with the same expression on your face. Is it just a replica of you that opens the door, and he has been made mild after witnessing something he cannot quite explain?

Despite your excommunication, the smell of your work clings to you the way a doubt clings. Urethane. Turpentine. Linseed. Oil paint. When Mink asks you, after you have kissed the tops of our heads and joined us at the dinner table, spilling whatever sauce is on it, 'So what did you do today?' you invariably say, 'I levitated.'

One night, after your usual exchange, Mink slaps you square across the jaw.

'Don't,' I say.

'Hit me back,' she orders.

You lift your arm. Immaculata gasps, 'Don't.' And then you pull Mink into you, quicksand, and you hold her until all of the lines that kept her taut break. She goes soft. Her face slumped in your chest, Mink laughs until she cries real tears — the tears she used to cry only for champions.

{ POSTCARD FROM OUTER SPACE }

echo!

A low hum and the island street lamps click on, coating the night green. The light of swamps. The smell of wet fur. Ten feet in front of me is a fox. Her furtive eyes, the yellow of an unvarnished trophy, are set on me. She does not flinch. So close, I can smell the gristle in her teeth. She walked ice floes last winter to get here, gliding and pouncing between them. A red streak, she rode them into shore. I listen to the rhythmic pull of her breath. A pendulum. It feels like a drawing in. I am fading, being carried off, to be spread through the woods in a hundred holes beneath the ground.

I shout and flail my arms. I jump up and down. In Darlington, you taught me: *When trapped in the woods and faced with a bear and the bear snorts, make yourself bigger than you are so that it does not confuse you with prey.* This is what I am doing. Making myself bigger than I am. The fox looks at me. I am foolish. She will not show her teeth and lunge at me, taking my throat with her, sinews stretched like a cat's cradle between us. She has other plans. And she is busy. *Come on.* She begins to trot, her body a sleek flare, and then she turns her head to see that I follow. I do. Along this strip of road, she leads me a few hundred feet to a clearing. *Always in the same untravelled clearing in the woods.* The street lamps click off. Night rushes in again, an iodine spill. The clearing blinks with fireflies. They are maniacs of light. The fox bounds between them. They illuminate my surroundings. I do not know whether she stays to watch, her eyes and the pulse of the bugs indistinguishable.

The pines are pulled back, slingshots with the wind. Two maples bow into each other, their tops bent heavily in conference like elders, like lovers. Beneath them, there is one square for the moon to burn through. It is lanced by shadow. It is the face of Finbar, his bones punching him out from the inside, other lives clambering for space. He is telling me to go. I tie Marta's rope between them. It is the width of three of my fingers, one of yours. Life must be caught up to. This is a moment that has been chasing me and finally I am alongside it. Vertigo. The stars come out. A million white knuckles. A nervous sky.

I kick off my boots, climb the tree and step up onto the rope. That quarter inch dare to the air. One foot. It is taut, braided sinews to the underside of my arches. I lift the other foot — standing distilled to such a fine point. I fall. I fall again and again. I fall, Immaculata would count, *sixty-one times whoa*, without ever taking a step forward. This last time, my stomach catches on something: a piece of glass, half-buried. I wince. It will become my second scar.

You have seventy-two. You would roll up a pant leg, slip off your boot, pull your shirt down below your shoulder and tell me their stories. Some are long and wide like flattened worms. Others are mashed and spread, desperate beggars. Some are small divots, darker than your skin, where teeth and corners dug into you. Still others look like zippers. Two look like eyes. Three are dark blue from leeches pulled off your toes. But on your left side, snaking over your lower ribs and splitting into a trident shape, is your most tremendous scar. Suffered in a fall when you were a rodeo king in High Level, Alberta, arm in the air, stomach pulled in, the hard shell of a crustacean. You told me you sewed that one yourself. This was the only night you drank. Now anyone would have pegged you for a drinker. Probably whisky and a dark ale. But this was your only dabble. Bourbon. Old Crow. You called it *rotgut*. You said it nearly killed you. Spent the next day retching on your hands and knees. I run my fingers over the mark of the stitches, too exaggerated, the seams too thick. This body is one you had to work to keep on.

Immaculata thought you made them up. She told me this once, rocking back and forth on her blistered heels, bottom lip sucked in under her teeth, her expression fretful; she did not know how to introduce me to the idea. It was a line out into the unknown. When she saw my response, she exclaimed with a consolatory smile, 'He is so clumsy Eugenia he is a total klutz think about it!' I called her a liar and she said, searching my face, 'I'll leave you alone excuse me,' and then, the human postscript, she added, 'That is not to say his stories are not true to him.'

Possessed now by precise strokes, I step onto the rope. With one foot and then the other, I stand. I lift my left foot – the empty air heaving around me – and I step forward. I do not fall. With that, the world loses its squares and its contours. It lengthens into the blurred landscape from a speeding train. Hurtling through, brain waves in sleep, the pace of the planet quivering – all shapes are stretched into vast lines of colour. I am drowned out. And turned to light. A lightness that is secret, a most vivid secret.

I reach the end. I linger there, my heart in my ears – the footsteps of an elephant. The tightrope is the darkroom, images suspended and becoming themselves before your eyes.

Around me, there is only the white puff of cottonwood seeds, floating like shrunken clouds. I am thousands of feet in the air and I am suddenly a giant. In the silence, I hear a line snap. It is the line between us. The one that bound me to you. *Snap*. And with that snap, a mysterious pool takes shape. It does not have any echo or reflection. It is indifferent. It is aloneness. Finally, aloneness.

{ POSTCARD FROM OUTER SPACE }

*1. a successful trip begins long before you
arrive at your destination.*

2. plan in advance.

*3. study relevant maps and literature
consider buying pocket-sized versions.*

*4. familiarize yourself with local customs
such as dress, food, religion and dating.*

5. choose sites to visit, e.g., shrines and arenas.

6. finalize itinerary.

*7. finalize travel arrangements and book
accommodation in advance.*

8. consult relevant dictionary.

*9. practice local phrases, e.g., what time is the bus?
do you have a vacancy? which way is east?
where is the nearest hospital?*

10. stock up on local currency.

11. pack lightly.

*12. once you arrive, find your local
tourist information office.*

This night, the fifth night, I dream about someone other than you.

Finbar stands at his dresser. A cockroach on a cufflink. The house is half-eaten by spiderwebs. Everything is under a hide of dust. The floorboards are splintered and buckled. I can hear his long yellow nails clacking against the pencil as he writes to me, tapping out a code. He folds the letter and seals the envelope with his tongue. Fried egg, Scotch, fish. He addresses it, stamps it, and then he looks through his mottled window. The pods are still there, burst by branches, gauze nests in the willows.

After all the women left Orphan Stadium to scream in their parents' living rooms, delivering Finbar's children with their linen nightgowns on, Finbar held a funeral for his penis. He made a paper boat, phallic in shape, and he set it off in the outdoor sink. Naked, he lit it on fire and thought he heard a dirge being sung. Then he returned indoors and he let the place rot. Himself too. There was no reason for upkeep, no bodies to steer into bed and impress. He spent his days writing longhand, his *Unofficial Auto-biography*, the empire collapsing around him. He needed a record of his life before the cataracts, those argent spaceships, took over his eyes completely.

Finbar steps outside. The house is a hulk in the wild. Fields stretch out around it, overgrown with the season. Grass lifts from the gravel, mohawking the road that leads to it. Scorched poles where torches once burned spot the ragged setting like matches snuffed out. Beside the kitchen window, propped open with a wooden spoon, cans are piled high. His dinners. Mostly asparagus. Some oysters. Vines and creepers, Orphan Stadium is being grown over. A plot untended. There is a hand-painted sign on the front lawn, faded now, that says VACANCY. Finbar put it up after his Queen died all those years ago. Now, in his slippers, smelling of sawdust, dead mice and woodsmoke, sauce in his beard, he checks the mailbox – just in case the girl had something to add. No. Empty. The only mail he has ever received here: birth announcements – cut and clipped neatly from the newspaper. All of them, sons. And none named for him.

The letter to the eighteen-year-old girl strains in his liver-spotted hand. Quaking, he slips it into the pocket of his silk bathrobe. Looking down, he sees that he is still wearing the note he pins to himself every night before falling asleep: NOT DEAD YET, PLEASE CHECK FOR PULSE OR MORTAL WOUND – having been taken to the mortician and pronounced dead and nearly buried three times already.

Sound of a match striking the air. And my name. 'Eugenia.' Finbar is not calling me. He is testing it on his property.

I wake up to something prodding my left side. It feels like a snout. Probably the last wild boar. 'What ho,' it says. I open my eyes. The sun is bright as a blister. A red stamp, it blights the shape above me, making it black. But I know that voice, those words like ancient shale, ostrich feathers, hops and grunts in a mouth. I wonder if the sun is his permanent backdrop.

'What ho,' I respond.

The man is wearing a diving suit. It shimmers wet. His dark hair drips. He holds a metal detector with a round disc at its base and presses it up against my breast pocket. Beeps come through the headphones that hang around his neck.

Mink told me that she had two hearts. One where a heart should be and another in her stomach. She put my hand on her stomach and I could feel a dull thud there. I imagined a baby in captivity and Mink confusing the baby with a surplus of love. My hand under hers, pulsing, she said that when I was a baby my skin was so soft it was tarantula skin.

'When did you touch a tarantula?'

'Before you.'

'What else did you do before me?'

'Everything.' She said *everything* like she was drinking it. 'Don't worry. You'll do everything too.'

We are in the sand dunes at the western end of the island, Hanlan's Point. I slept here, the tall grasses shooting into a fence around me, a net below. The man hoists me up. I land in the hollow of his chest where, if he lay flat, he would collect rainwater. The capped teeth. The beginnings of a beard. His hair is longer than I remember and his nose is a nose that has been broken more than once.

'How did you break your nose?'

'I didn't break it. Somebody else did.'

'Why?'

'He said he didn't want me to forget him.'

'He must have said it a few times.'

'He did.'

'Why didn't you duck his punches?'

'If he was looking at my nose he wouldn't look in my pockets.'

The man's jaw is strong. With it, he could play a villain in a movie. But not with the rest of his face. It is too gentle. His eyes are an opalescent grey, the colour of a tent left out of doors too long.

'There was a store here on this end of the island. Durnan's Boat House. It was built over the water. A lot fell through the floorboards.' The man wears bags around his hips. One is heavily weighted with rusty square-headed nails, pocket knives and bottle caps. A single coin in the other. He holds it out for me to see. 'Copper goes green. Silver goes black.' Blackened, the face is nearly rubbed off. It reminds me of your portraits tied up, a parcel on the curb, the weather vulturing them, the paintings taking on the bruises and the galaxies of mould.

'You're a treasure hunter.'

'Though when I walk into the water everyone thinks I'm trying to kill myself.'

'Has anyone ever tried to stop you?'

'No.' He is not perplexed.

Lying in the dunes is a pair of roller skates, black with red stoppers. The man slings them over his shoulder. I hit the sand from my suit. It sounds like an hourglass. Patting down my breast pocket, I feel there something the size of a thimble, a glass eye. I will see to it when I am alone.

'I made the pie.'

'No fire.'

'Not this time. I'll feed you.'

'You live here.'

'Since the day I was born.'

'What about your accent?'

'I was away for a long time. Now I'm home.'

My stomach groans. I place my hand over it, parting my suit jacket, and there, the size of a minnow and rust in colour, is the blood dried from my fall onto the glass. It looks like a keyhole. Before he lifts the tail of my shirt, the man says, 'Excuse me, I am a gentleman.' He circles the cut with his finger, skin rough as burlap. 'You are hurt.' The pull in my jaw.

Without saying anything more, the man picks me up and piggybacks me northeast and over the bridge to Algonquin Island. He is not wearing shoes. He does not look down once, feet fast as hummingbirds. On the way, he stops, puts me down, turns around, wipes his hand against his wetsuit and extends it. We shake.

'Samuel Station.'

'Eugenia.'

'Eugenia. Samuel Station.'

'Eugenia Stunt Ledoux.'

'Stunt.' He repeats the word as if it were an unopened box in his mouth. 'I am pleased to make your acquaintance.'

'And yours.'

Our eyes meet like we are duellers in the woods who have forgotten to shoot each other.

I say, 'I think we're the only people awake.'

He lifts me onto his back again. Through my shirt, I can feel his spine. A new set of buttons, it runs down the centre of my chest, shortcut to a dissection.

13. have a backup plan.

.

Samuel Station lives in a houseboat. It is a cedar-planked affair, thirty feet long and ten feet wide. It floats under a stand of cottonwood. In blue cursive, it tells me its name, the *Station*. I imagine its voice – a drawl, almost elderly, it has so much gravel in it. Ducks swim the surrounding water. They are teenage ducks: petulant, dirty and coming together in the shape of a wishbone. The *Station* has been well cared for. If it were in miniature, it would be on display amidst tie pins, badges and cigar boxes on a mantel above a roaring fire.

With me still on his back, Samuel follows the tilted dock to the *Station*. He then steps onto the slender deck of his boat, spattered with shadow, leaves above bristling silver. Cottonwood seeds fall to the ground, confetti in slow motion. He lets me down delicately, a sleeper, the swoon of water below. I adjust my stance. A ladder runs between the deck and the roof. Samuel climbs it. Stopping halfway, a buccaneer hanging from a mast, he leans out and says, 'Please. Sit.' I do. In a wingback chair, its velvet worn. A pair of black boots beneath it. Polished, leather, steel toes poking out.

You had one scar that was ugly. Your left big toe. When your adoptive mother, Plump Marie, saw that toe, that disquieted lump of flesh, its nail worn right off, the flesh bunched and yellow beneath, she lit a prayer candle and cried for a week, saying that your feet were rooming-house feet and that it would be her fault if you ever ended up in one. You had not wanted to bother her, she gave you so much already, letting you sleep between her breasts when you were a newborn, the size of a pint of blueberries, so you fastened your too-small boots every morning, and walked, face screwed into the wind. Passersby thought you were worrying a point when it was really just pain, your first encounter with pain and all it had to offer.

You called Plump Marie your *second mother* when your *first mother* disappeared twenty minutes after delivering you, the night of Kapuskasing's fiercest snowstorm, in her baby-blue hospital gown, bare feet, toes painted red, a single leather suitcase in hand. She climbed into a Cadillac that purred black between the snowdrifts. She left behind a pair of white high heels that the nurses all agreed were inappropriate for a woman who knew she would become a mother that night. The nurses measured the baby and then, not able to help themselves, they measured the high heels beside him. Twenty-one inches. Six inches. The nurses clapped their palms to their cheeks, vaudevillian shock. The mother was tall enough without shoes like that. And, they whispered over the baby, *sexy*.

The only thing you knew about your first mother was that she had the name of an Italian movie.

Samuel Station jumps from the bottom rung of the ladder, a beet in his hand. Its broad-veined leaves spill out, bouquet for an asylum. His fingers are crumbed with dirt.

'The leaf will bind your wound.'

'Where did you learn that?'

'The Ural Mountains. A weather station.' He looks sternly at the cut.

'You have a garden on your roof?'

'Just beets. Though one day I hope for a horse.'

We pass the vestibule: in it, shovels, sieves, his roller skates, a second metal detector and a bow and arrow.

'Have you ever shot anything?'

'Yes.' Pulling open two sliding doors, 'Welcome.'

The houseboat is narrow. If Immaculata were here and she stretched out her arms, a woman on a clifftop, it would fit her twice across. Cedar, it is reminiscent of a glory box, filled with ancestral jewellery. From the ceiling hang hundreds of rings. Suspended by dark thread, they flicker and twirl in the midday light. Tiny acrobats could swing from them, their backs bent, their slow arcs and contractions through space.

Following Samuel, I duck between them. The rings are silver and gold, some embedded with gemstones, others finely scored. He picks up a nub of metal. 'My jeweller's mark.' It is the size of a fingertip. Now I understand why he was salvaging from the beach.

In one corner is Samuel's worktable. On its surface, in loose order: acorns, an envelope of gold dust spilled open, a watch-maker's drill, a surgeon's pliers, cuttlefish bone for casting, a lave, a ring mandrel, a rawhide mallet, rolling mills, files, a toothbrush, tweezers, sandpaper, glittering hills of sapphires, rubies and diamonds. Old tobacco tins store jewels: children's signet rings, pendants, watches and broaches. Lined up beside them are albums thick with coins. I flip through the weighty pages. A meticulous hand has labelled each one, where it was found and its approximate value. Samuel sells nothing. It is the act of seeing what is not readily apparent that propels him.

A blowtorch is hung against the wall. Below it, a gold ring. Washing the beet, Samuel says, without looking up, 'It cracked last night when I was finishing it. First time in a long time.'

Two windows are carved into the houseboat's sides. They are covered in nautical maps to temper the sun, which, in the *Station*, would otherwise be the sun of the desert. Immaculata would want the whole thing under an umbrella. Samuel, the spark of his skin too. There is also a window on the roof – a pyramid jutting up between the bulbs. Stippled with dirt, it makes the light in the boat that of a late afternoon. Samuel could eat breakfast by candlelight without being accused of eccentricity.

Later, he will tell me that this window was a hole when he found the boat eight years ago beached in a junkyard and looking like the world's oceans had dried up. Samuel loved the boat. He paid his nose for it, his front teeth too, having stolen keys, lock combinations and the only food that would subdue the German shepherds that roamed the yard – the owner's dinner.

Against the eastern wall is a single bunk hanging twelve feet above the living space on a wooden foundation. It is a bed for a monk, so close to the ceiling that Samuel could not spring up in a nightmare without banging his head. Hand-fashioned rungs lead up to it. They are what he balances on in the mornings to make his bed. White sheet. Red blanket, black stripes. Single pillow. A book tucked under it. Always the same one.

Below the bunk, a saddlebag tacked to the wall that could be fitted over the hump of a dromedary and ridden across the Arabian desert. Three wrought-iron pegs: a yellow raincoat and bib overalls hang from one, thick fur hat on top. Beside it, suspenders, the shirt and wool pants Samuel was wearing when we first met. White long johns on the third, moccasins beneath. Samuel is a man of systems and sure preferences. He thrives on the economy of space. He prints his initials in his clothing, a habit leftover from the house he grew up in. It feels like a tribute to his mother. He hides his socks. This, a tribute too.

In the centre of the room is a couch. Stacks of books raise its feet. It looks like Samuel, in collared cloak, lifted it from the court of Louis XVI, all turquoise and gold silk brocade, mahogany claws curled for traction against the wide plank floor, and carried it through centuries – a thief's portage – home. There should be a prostitute on it, face lead-oxide-whited over, Marie Antoinette hairdo, snoring intermission.

The western wall is a built-in bookshelf crammed with titles, piles laid crookedly upon other piles. Between them are small objects: the letter S in lead type, bars pulled from a xylophone, a horseshoe, an ostrich egg, a silver camel and boxing gloves. I pick up *The Small Lenormand Divinatory Card Game According to the Simplified Method Admirably Devised by Mademoiselle Lenormand.*

'Do you want to know the future?'

'Yes.'

He grins. He is missing some of his side teeth. 'Every night I dream the boat is sinking.' Samuel has met all of the emotions but only really recognized two of them as his own: seriousness and thrills. 'We are all destined for the bottom.'

Records lean up against a record player. David Bowie's *Hunky Dory* faces out. I read the spines of the books: Cugle's *Practical Navigation, The Compleat Angler, Let's Have an Encounter, The Book of Miso, The New Science of Skin and Scuba Diving, Larousse Gastronomique.* A number of heavy volumes in languages I do not recognize. Their letters are the contortions of insects. A strong wind would knock all of them to the floor.

Two bowls, two mugs, two sets of chopsticks.

'Were you expecting me?'

'Not even close.'

Beside the galley kitchen, there is a banquet table. It has been sawed and rebuilt to fit the space. The portion cut away forms the kitchen counter where Samuel stands drying the beet leaf in a towel that looks to be shrunken wool. He has the posture of a pharaoh. His motions are purposeful and exacting. He is a man who rarely gets lost. Or caught.

'Could you move the *Station*?'

'I could. It has two giant engines. But I never did get the steering wheel. It was the one part I couldn't find.'

'Maybe the owner swallowed it.'

'He did have quite the throat.'

Strung across the kitchen are lines of sausages curing, banners of hot peppers drying out and blocks of cheese aging into parmesan. Clear bottles of homemade grappa sit on a shelf above the sink. Beside them, a wooden crate is nailed into the wall with three boxes marked MISC., RECIPES and GOOD LUCK. A wash basin and, above it, a razor, a bar of soap and a towel worn at the edges. On top of the gas stove is the raspberry pie and, beside it, a loaf of fresh molasses bread. They are both caving in. 'I am a terrible baker,' Samuel says. 'Too much measuring. I have patience but not when I'm hungry.'

Still in his wetsuit, Samuel gestures toward the couch. 'Please.' I sit. 'Le Roi.'

'Pardon?'

'Le Roi. I name all of my furniture. The couch is the King. That guitar, Two-String Johnny. The table, Horst P. Horst.' He lifts the end of my shirt. 'My tools: Liberty Valance, Loudon, Nina, Stan, Tomboy, Leopard, Butch, the Overlord, the Undertaker.' He laughs, eyebrows shooting up, a tick of amazement. 'You are the first person to know that.' He dabs at the wound with a cloth, and then lays the beet leaf down, cool and damp. 'You will need a stitch, Eugenia. Or two.' He gives me a second leaf, taps his heart and then points to mine. He returns to the kitchen and fills the kettle, turning his back so that I can unbutton my shirt and lay the beet leaf down. Against my skin, it is a flag pulled from stormwater.

Samuel gives me a bowl of white broth with carrots and seaweed and green onions, some sweet bread and a piece of raspberry pie. He retreats to the back of the *Station*, peeling off his wetsuit and pulling on his clothes while I eat.

'This is the best meal I have ever had.'

'Because you slept outside last night. That makes everything taste better.'

When I am finished, he kneels down in front of me with the box labelled GOOD LUCK in one hand and a bottle of Scotch in the other. From the box, he pulls a needle and a spool of dark thread. He passes me the Scotch. Lagavulin. 'Single malt. Please.' I take a sip, having never tasted alcohol before. The Scotch drags its long hot fingers down my throat. I cough. I take another sip. And another. My ears feel full of water. My eyes too.

'Ready?'

I nod. He splashes Scotch on the cut. As I look up, the ceiling sways, the rings are dangled by hypnotists. His blowtorch to the needle, I feel its first prick and, not one for pain, I faint.

For a moment, I am under Immaculata's bed and I am revolving.

{ POSTCARD FROM OUTER SPACE }

e,

the earth is so harmless from here.
i can blot it out with my thumb.
yes, it is a marble.
yes, it is a child's toy.
yes, it is punctuation.
the end.

your s

Next morning, I am standing in front of our former home, heart loose in my throat, waiting for word from Finbar. The sky, pendulous above, its owl eye flashing, is bottle-glass green. Soon the air will break apart into droplets. Mr. and Mrs. Next Door have already landscaped our front lawn, tailoring the overgrown shrubs into cones and spirals. Pink and blue flowers dot the dirt below, discarded pompoms. The house, once a weathered white, is now painted purple with pink trim. It is suddenly the headquarters for the glee club, and it taunts, cheerily: *Just try to burn me down.* The windowsills are crowded with figurines, plaid curtains hanging behind them patterned like party napkins.

In front of the house are our bedrooms. The contents of our dressers, our desks, our books, our barrettes, our board games are laid out on tables, prices stuck to them. Most everything is less than one dollar. Except Mink's hairbrush. It is five. Her wig: eight. Even Immaculata's folder labelled DEATH is for sale.

Mr. Next Door sits on a lawn chair, today's newspaper open in his lap. He is wearing a windbreaker, hood up and pulled tight, the knot tied by Mrs. Next Door double-looped under his chin.

'I am so sorry,' he offers, too solemn, and then waves the paper as though he is being attacked by hornets and it will clear the air.

I look away from him, his anguished face – what is loss but loss split again into more loss? Up the street, I catch sight of a white pigeon flying in through Leopold's bedroom window just as it is being boarded up, the other windows already covered in planks and nailed tight. Inside, with matching butter knives, Leopold and Immaculata scrape the dirty bumper stickers from the bedposts, the lampshades, the entertainment unit. Later, they will build a pyre in the backyard and burn most everything.

Immaculata will place the mask she has sewn onto Leopold so that he will not take in any smoke. Tying it around his mouth, she will cough explanation: 'It just wouldn't be good for you cough cough.' Together, they watch his old life burn. The flames remind him of the only time he saw his mother wrestle. In the morning, there will be the mark of fire in the grass. They will pick up the blackened remnants, the logs like stacking blocks until they break apart, ashes under their fingernails. And then they will hold hands.

The dogs love Immaculata instantly.

The postman approaches just as Mrs. Next Door glides out in full rain gear with a stack of our orange tarpaulins. 'Rain, every garage sale's worst enemy!' she announces. She looks at me and then quickly to the ground like it is yawning open into a cauldron and soon it will swallow her. The postman approaches, stops in front of the house, combs through his pile and then continues on his way, nothing to deliver. The smell of defeat. The birds come out, frenzied in their song. A storm is set to hit. The three of us stand there, not quite staring at each other.

{ POSTCARD FROM OUTER SPACE }

eugenius,

the newborn stars, you can tell they are newborn
because they glow scarlet halos
with hydrogen announcing themselves
2500 light-years from the earth.
but what i really need to tell you is this:
fixed points are a fiction.
fixed points are a fiction.
fixed points are a fiction.

s.

The rain skips off the polished deck of the ferry. It stampedes the roof. And then it becomes so heavy that, inside, the white and blue walls glisten wet as though the passengers before us were licking them. Across from me, the high shriek of pleasure from a portly woman in an apron giggling at a joke made by a man whose arm she grabs for a moment. She steadies herself. He carries a pair of flippers. Looking back at the city, raindrops snaking across the window, the rain appears like pins on a map and the city is being sewn shut.

I race to the *Station*, tongue out, dusk sky in torrents, the rain, a curtain, pulled sideways by the wind that I run through again and again. Breathless. Knocking. Translucent. Everything is pearls.

'Where can we swim?'

Samuel Station takes my hand and we run down to the channel. Along the way, cabbages have broken through the bottom of a paper bag. Leaves flayed purple, gleaming. Fresh enough to eat. The islanders have retreated to their cottages. The power goes out. The beams of flashlights, the glimmer of candles. Some children dance between the cottages in bright raincoats, pockets heavy with water, habitats for goldfish. Immaculata told me that goldfish grow depending on the space they are accorded. I see the children walking down to the lake and emptying their pockets there, returning day after day to wade into the water and to stroke their giant fish, their hearts swelling and becoming nearly unbearable in their chests.

Samuel takes off his shirt and his pants and stands naked before me. His body is more muscular than I imagined. It lies in long strips, slender portions. He bows and laughs. I laugh too, rain coming down around us in gulps and needles. He glistens.

Dared, I take off my jacket, my pants, my shirt, my undershirt, my underwear. I too am naked. Samuel runs his fingers over the stitch of my new scar and then he stands back. He looks at me for a long time. I cock my hip, hoping for the illusion of curves. We laugh again — my boy's body, the body that never flourished.

We slip down the boulders and the moss that clings to them. We reach the shoreline — stones, branches and froth. We find a still pool. Slip in. Quake and pant. The dying light stripes us. Our faces, like the banks of the channel, are streaked in fins and ivories, making us exotic, shimmering creatures. Evolution. We are buoyant. We find each other's hands and press our bodies together, my legs finding his hips, his mouth finding mine. Lips thick like a foreign script. All the desire that has been in me, scouring the earth for a contour, for a place to plunge myself into, rushes to the fore. We kiss for a long time, tasting each other's interiors — what we have known, what we have eaten, what we have loved; all of the stories borne by smell, by taste, lying dormant, are drawn out of my mouth and into his. He dives beneath the surface and takes my nipples in his mouth, between his teeth, a gentle bite, and me, floating on my back, his tongue tracing my belly, my thighs, and then inside me, his hands holding my hip bones, I move with the sway of the water. To be loved is to be picked up, a stone, to be smoothed out. To be loved is to be given the space to explode in.

I come down to him, to his wet neck, his collarbone, his chest, his sex, a swan in my throat, I take him whole, and there I taste the languages, the dwellings, the oceans; all that he has been is inside me now. I am marked. A monument, glorious defeat, I am done. I lift myself up and pull him inside me, perfect pain, and we are still there for a long time, our bodies full and tight with the wet of each other and the wet of the water, the rain pelting the surface, he pulls the ends of my hair and sucks the lake from them, our mouths fall together. I start to move, a deep slow fit, this is the act of becoming, our bodies sink until they are the speed of the tremors in the centre of the earth. We mend each other. He tips his head back and he cries. My skin is seconds old.

A long quiet. Between the wind and the water both raging now, we are weightless, extinguished.

Samuel takes my hand and kisses the centre of my palm. I have never been kissed there. Then, he fills his lungs and he dives down into the channel, staying below for what feels like three minutes. I tread water, with him somewhere amidst the bicycles covered in barnacles, the church organ and the shipwreck – a Swedish fishing boat called the *Baltic Belle* built at the turn of the last century. Samuel told me that on a winter day you can lie on the ice and see her every black rib.

Just as my breath becomes skittish, spikes and flutters, he returns with a fish in his hand. It flops frantic, folding itself over and over again. He holds it above his head and shakes it back and forth, quickly snapping its backbone. Samuel is so steady that from the shore you would swear he was standing on the bottom.

'A yellow perch,' he says, eyelashes wet triangles, presenting the fish. 'I am going to cook for you.'

We come up out of the river, and there we see that I have grown hips and breasts. He lets his mouth fall over them again before carrying me into his home, the fish, gold and dark green, dangling from his other hand.

June 15, 1981. Mrs. Next Door and I are on the front lawn of 101 Dunn Avenue playing tug-of-war with the air, until she implores, 'Please go away now, go away, we don't want any trouble here.' She has not made many sales. The tables are still mostly full, the racks of clothing and assorted displays seemingly untouched. I don't know which is worse: being for sale or not being sold.

'I just want to know if anything has come in the mail.'

'I have already told you, dear, no.'

I browse like a thug, making it clear that I am not leaving.

'Some rain,' she offers.

'Some rain.'

'Three whole days.'

I handle the merchandise: Mink's audition tape, her old headshots, her black tights and turtlenecks, my white sunglasses frames, Immaculata's baby blanket.

'You know, there's a cat buried in the backyard.'

'Oh.'

'Under the apple tree. Her name was Urszula Minor. She was tailless. If you're desperate, you could sell her too.'

Mrs. Next Door titters and then she takes a quick peek behind her. Mr. Next Door draws the party-napkin curtains closed. Mink's water-skiing photo, Immaculata's collection of embalmed rodents, Finbar one thousand feet above Niagara Falls, cut from the library book and smoothed out, it is all for sale — a sign propped between:

BARGAINS BARGAINS BARGAINS

I know that Mrs. Next Door is lying. I know that there is something for me here. I think about throwing a fit, falling and flexing on the grass, Mrs. Next Door hovering above me, pleading, 'Don't bite your tongue.' Instead, the smallest striptease in the world, I lift the end of my shirt and show her my fresh scar.

'Ow.'

She draws in a long breath. 'Poor dear.' And then she comes so close I could bite her arm. She smells of jam and glue. I can see where her liquid makeup stops, tan-coloured before her hairline. A perm growing out, Marta would call it *russet*, her hair is pulled back with two bronze bobby pins that hang a little bit. Eyes on the scar, she tells it, 'Don't you move.'

I look up the street. Immaculata knew things about me that you didn't. She knew that when I was afraid I saw panthers sprinting up the stairs behind me. She knew that I liked names with five syllables best. Hers was one. Im-ma-cu-la-ta. Yours was the other. Sheb-Woo-ly-Le-doux. When I told her that I had seen a ghost at the end of my bed, and that she was bald and had no teeth, she just stood there not haunting me or making any noise, just staring at me, Immaculata made me promise, 'If she visits again Euge get me.' But the ghost never came back.

Sa-mu-el Sta-tion. Five syllables.

Inside their boarded-up house, Immaculata is preserving a red squirrel. Slats of light come through the windows as if she is always standing beside a film projector. Leopold watches her. His face is so radiant, it melts. After she makes lunch, Immaculata brushes her teeth while she pees, as she used to do, and Leopold sits on the edge of the bathtub, as I used to do. He thinks he sees her blossom and then die and then he panics that she will leave him. He says 'No' aloud.

'What is *no*?'

'Will you ever leave me?'

'No.'

He is comforted, though he still wishes for *forever*.

Mrs. Next Door dips a cotton ball in Immaculata's rubbing alcohol and then pushes it, astringent, against my skin.

It stings. 'Ow.'

'I'm sorry.'

'I don't think it's infected.'

'Just to be sure.'

She retracts her hand and chimes, 'All done.' Something about the timbre of her voice sets her off. Her head fills with sirens. A stitch of agony sprouts between her eyes. Together, we sink in the damp grass, possessions grouped around us, listening to the *plink plink* of construction nearby. Mrs. Next Door pulls me to her. She smells like Mink's closet. I realize then that she is wearing all of Mink's clothes. Because they do not fit, she has had to layer them to cover herself: a sweater on top of a shirt on top of a dress on top of a leotard. Her arms are long and bone-thin. A praying mantis. They tackle me, her hug too strong. I try to tear away but she will not let me.

So I surrender. Ear against Mink's black cardigan, cashmere, I listen to her ragged breath, its effort; she is resuscitating something. Dew beads the grass below us. The world is made up of points, and while we can see each other from a distance, up close we are all indecipherable.

Mrs. Next Door suddenly steps back and reaches into the pocket of Mink's sweater – where the rope once was, the knife, the bags that captured your studio. Behind her, my nightgown stirs, discounted, on a hanger. She hands me an envelope.

'Is there anything else?' I ask.

She shakes her head, 'No. Time to go,' and I watch her walk back into the house. She locks the door behind her.

*M*s. *Eugenia Ledoux.*
Finbar's hand.

Inside the envelope is a key with a black vinyl tag marked 12 and a map to a motel called the Bedou Inn. The map is hand-drawn. If this were a war, its artist would be a prized draftsman. There is a note asterisked in the bottom corner: *check-in 3 p.m.* It looks to have been formulated during turbulence. Finbar, his eyes washed-out discs, turning the edges of everything into bathwater. The map tells me that the motel is on the Lake Shore. East. Here, in Toronto. When I expected to be boarding a train, coat brass-buttoned to my neck, travelling for entire days, climbing mountain passes, breathing frost and leaving time zones, when I expected the bite of Alaska, the Bedou Inn is probably only an hour by streetcar. This is disorienting, my projected journey so foreshortened. A dog barks from a rooftop above me. It sounds like collegial agreement. This is when I notice that there is no postage on the envelope. It was delivered by hand.

When I leave the *Station* this morning to go to 101 Dunn Avenue for the last time, mail or no mail, Samuel is asleep in the middle of the floor, his arms and legs starfished open, lungs lifting and falling like soft cymbals. He talks in his sleep, a language that I do not know. The consonants ponderous in his mouth, I press my ear against it and experience the most gentle form of possession. He is wearing his wool socks; I can see where he darned them on the heel.

We pull the mattress down from his bunk and we spend three days there, rain seeping in through the glass pyramid above us. The *Station* rising with the water level, Samuel checks the bilge pump and loosens the anchor lines. He plays records and he dances with the pluck and possibility of a colt. He pours Scotch for me in a mug and then adds ice from a bag labelled Iceberg Ice. We clink our mugs together and propose movements: *The Tenderness Movement! The Retirement Movement! The Movement Movement!* I watch him in still lifes: *Man Waltzing Half-Naked. Man Clowning as Though for a Photograph. Man Snagging Heart Like Soft Paw.*

He strokes my feet, birds flying out of corners. I take him in my mouth – the flashbulb of temper, the devotion of strangers. He tells me, fingers in my hair, my mouth open against his collarbone, tasting salt and blowtorch and gold, his thigh hard between mine like the top of a fence, 'I believe in the skills of one's hand above all else. Technology is about to rule us, Eugenia, but when it implodes, these skills will be all that matter.' He never abbreviates my name. We feed each other with our fingertips. Beets and fish and bread and pie until there is nothing left. We stumble and interrupt, pulling each other from the mattress to the kitchen counter to a squat by the door, speaking to an ankle bone, sharp like a scythe, the crevasse behind an ear, eyes squeezed shut and wet in corners, the down on the back of a neck, the birthmark beside a belly button. We have been separated for too long and we have to rush to tell each other things and we do not want to forget one. We refuse sleep. If we succumb to it, we could lose each other in the night. Samuel Station describes tracking wolves and living for one year in a weather station and how a woman told him once, 'You are so solitary.' And she was right. He is solitary. His worst nightmare is to be in a room full of people. Unless they are dancing.

And then he asks, as I climb the first rung of the ladder and he comes up behind me, forehead between my shoulder blades, hands rough on my hips, I tilt them back toward him, body quivering, the needle of a compass, 'Do you think that we are really alone in this world or are we twins who eventually find each other, completing puzzles?'

Not looking at him, I say, 'I don't know yet.'

Stepping off the tilted dock, first time on land in three days, I adjust my stance. Water laps the shore behind me, an obsession. I recall the sound of the metal detector against my heart. I reach into my breast pocket and fish out a gold necklace. Marta's locket. I see her tearing it from her neck, so hard she breaks the skin. I open it. No photograph. Blank canvas cut to fit. No self-portrait. You could never stand still long enough to finish one. You explained that your own face just made you want to run. I throw the locket into the lagoon. A small shock against the water. Your limbs striking the surface of a pond. The locket will sink and travel, be found one morning and melted down.

I walk south from the streetcar stop toward the Bedou Inn, the city thinning out around me. A reverend hurries by me. His skin tobacco-brown, hair dyed margarine-yellow, white boots and a black hat, a suitcase on wheels that won't quite close because of the hotplate nudging its zipper. In his pipe-cleaner arms, he holds out a cat for an aegis. It is Sirloin the cat, with his one lazy eye, the sign still on his back:

> *I have been abandoned.*
> *Please be kind.*

As they pass, the reverend mutters to me, 'God works, God works' – not like God works in a factory or God works in a disco but like God was broken and now God works.

You told me once that you nearly killed yourself but that at the last moment God saved you. You knew that you had to die outside the house so as not to scar us forever, so you called a taxi and you opened the passenger door, noose already looped around your shoulder. 'Rosedale Ravine, man.' You planned on hanging yourself from a 130-year-old tree in the place you found most beautiful in the city. You had looked. And, like a dog, you wanted to die alone in the woods. You thought being alone was brave – more brave than being with other people. You tied the noose while watching Clint Eastwood play Marshal Jedediah Cooper in *Hang 'Em High*. Taking note of the technique for both of us, parroting a prisoner in the hole, *it snaps your neck like a dried-out twig*, and soon after demanding, 'Unlearn that, unlearn that right now, Eugenia!' On the way to the ravine, a fog descended upon the city, blurring it and then hiding it. It became impossible to find anything. Cars put on their blinkers and then finally pulled over, obsolete robots. An open road, and the taxi driver saw it as adventure. And for some reason, he wanted to impress you. Maybe it was your eyes. You had fighter eyes, Clint Eastwood eyes. He persevered until apologizing, 'I could try to get you back home.' But then he could not do that either. Finally he stopped the taxi and let you out, saying, 'Good luck, man.' He did not charge you, which struck you as chivalrous, and maybe even lucky. You stepped out onto the curb. You thought maybe this was heaven. Heaven is so private – you cannot really see anything but your own hands in heaven. And then you looked down and saw that you were standing on a path and so you followed it and vowed that its end would be your home. When you pushed open the front door, you were looking at the three of us looking at you, noose looped around your shoulder. You were home and this is when you started to believe in miracles.

{ POSTCARD FROM OUTER SPACE }

stunt,

you cannot move between two points
without a belief in the other end.

your,
s

The Bedou Inn is a small motel, twelve rooms in total, located where the Lake Shore meets Cherry Street. Rectangular, built of brick, it is reminiscent of a freight car dislocated from a train. The motel is beside the empty site where the circus pitches its blue-and-yellow-striped tent when it comes to town and people weep under it because they see other versions of their kind in flight. A mess of rail yards around it, mostly industrial land, one diner kitty-corner called the Canary, the smell of grease and sugar, OPEN glowing in its window.

Room 12 is the corner room and the receptionist tells me in a sharply articulate voice, 'It is the only suite here, the only suite at the Bedou Inn.'

Sitting behind a teak desk on a chair that swivels, reading glasses strung round her neck, the receptionist wears a midnight-blue taffeta gown that gathers at her waist. She slept in it. No stockings. It is just too hot. She wears black ankle boots that point at the ends. They look to be too big, perhaps even a man's; she stuffs the toes to make them fit. Her hair is thick and grey, to the shoulders, and evokes the heaps on the beautician's floor. Her body is an elegy. A cat balance-beams the edge of the desk. Another one sits by the door. And another sleeps, curled, a closed fist, in her lap. The air is full of dander. A standing fan in the corner makes it tremble.

Books are piled high around her. They are imitations of her face: opened, read and closed too many times.

'I used to have a lover who read Rumi to me in translation.' She lights a cigarette even though one is already burning in the overflowing ashtray, the waft of sweet wine rising with the smoke. 'But he died.'

'Are those his boots?'

'Yes.' She laugh-coughs. 'He slept with them on for a year. So that they fit perfectly. His feet. Not mine.' She laugh-coughs again. It is the sound of a tuba under water.

A tattered black velour curtain hangs behind her. Its bottom is fringed white with cat hair. I can make out a cot covered in Indian prints and what appears to be a green budgie flying free. It is her one wild thought. She would have taught her cats to go against their natures and not kill the bird. 'It is so rare to meet three-dimensional people these days, don't you think?'

'Yes.'

'Like they are extinct.' She strokes the cat in her lap, her touch darkening its coat for a second. 'Are they?'

'No.'

'That's a relief.'

'May I ask you please who made the arrangements?'

'I haven't a clue.' She huffs booze and bites her teeth together to stop herself from saying anything more and then she looks at me, eyes blue as the marrow of fire, moves her hand like she is lifting a heavy canvas off herself and her tamed cats. Ta da. She is dismissing me. I close the door to the sound of her muted chatter, finishing our conversation with her cats, Rumi, 'We are going to sky, who wants to come with us?'

There is a milk truck parked in front of Room 2. Otherwise the lot is empty. Some silver trash bins and a single shoe. If only the shoes had agreed on a meeting place. Three plastic chairs are set out between the rooms. Once people sat on them and read to each other.

As I push the key into the lock, I wonder what will await me there in the gloom: a crepuscular Finbar in sultry repose feeding himself grapes, a baby tiger at his feet, or you, a bag messily packed with clothes that will no longer fit me?

Your last night at home, when you joined us at the dinner table, folding a green bean into your mouth before sitting down, Mink asked you as she always did, 'So what did you do today?'

You answered as you always did. 'I levitated.'

For the first time, she said, 'Show us.'

'I can't.' You explained, 'I have to be alone to do it.'

'And where do you go when you levitate?'

'Nowhere. Yet.'

'But then —'

'But then, I am going to levitate into outer space. I need to see where I came from. Don't you?'

I sat there letting the question echo sepulchral in my bones. And then Mink said, 'Thank you, Sheb.'

Without the war between them, our parents were suddenly weightless. We hurried into their laps, sinkers keeping them in place.

'But what about us what will we do when you're in outer space what will we do without you our family would be uneven,' Immaculata pleaded.

'I'll send postcards,' and then you winked. Newborns contort their faces in sleep, practicing to win their parents' love. I gave you my most convincing face.

'Did you hear that?' you asked.

'No.'

'A bell is ringing.' And then you looked at me with a love in your eyes, but the love could have belonged to anyone.

I open the door to Room 12. Propped on its kickstand is your bicycle. The black frame, broken toe clips, rearview mirror duct-taped to the yellow handlebars, the wooden Canadian Butter box bungee-corded onto the rear rack. You are not here. But your bicycle is. I run my hands over it. The grease of the chain. You have not been on it for days – nothing of you lingers, nothing.

The walls are covered with framed needlepoints. So clustered together, I can barely make out the bold floral wallpaper behind them. You came home with a suitcase full of these once after a three-week stay in the hospital. You were wearing socks with the hospital name and address printed on them. I remember the stink in the corridors: hot food and industrial cleaner, and that you wanted to host picnics on the weekends because there were more suicides on the weekends, and if people were together on a blanket, sharing sandwiches, they might forget to kill themselves. Your needlepoints were all portraits of other patients, their pupils bumpy to the touch. The doctors told you, 'Even here you try to be the best.'

A silk nightgown is laid out on the bed. A toothbrush, toothpaste and ivory comb are on the bathroom counter. The bath is drawn. I skim my hand through the water. Still hot. Lavender oil. In the bar fridge, there is a block of cheese wrapped in wax paper, a jar of olives and a corked bottle of white wine. One linen napkin. French bread on the desk with a knife, grainy mustard and maple cutting board. Samuel told me that scissors make the divots in French bread; he was a cook for bush camps near Nanaimo and baked twenty loaves at a time. He ordered flour in fifty-pound bags. He stored vegetables underground in a dugout called a cache, and mashed hundreds of potatoes with bags over his feet because to do them by hand would have taken too long. The firefighters were hungry. Once, he had to give all of his French bread to a black bear mad with starvation. The berries were late and so the bear stalked the camp. Samuel could not believe how much the bear liked his bread. And that it did not kill him.

Otherwise the room is made up of the standard fixtures: a double bed, a suitcase stand, a rack with hangers, a Gideon Bible in a bedside table. The suite part of the room consists of a couch in an alcove. I check the drawers, between the mattresses, under the pillows, but there is no note, and there is no second map.

Samuel tucked the same book under his pillow every night, the idea being that the contents would drift up and lodge in his mind. There was a prophet who learned everything this way. The Sleeping Prophet. And Samuel thought: try. *Teaching a Stone to Talk.* Annie Dillard. He had to keep elastics around it or he would lose all of its pages. Sections were starred and underlined, some drawings beside them; this made me think he had spent time in prison, and there, in his cell, he had only this book.

Reading it, he said, we had to wear 3-D glasses. We put them on — one red square, one blue over our eyes. My head in his lap, the smell of two bodies rooted together in the air, he read his favourite part to me early one morning when there was no food left in the *Station* but a small envelope of saffron picked by Mennonites. We filled our mouths with the expensive flower. 'Could two live under the wild rose, and explore by the pond, so that the smooth mind of each is as everywhere present to the other, and as received and as unchallenged as falling snow?'

'We could put raven feathers behind our ears and call ourselves the chief of something.'

'Ravens.'

'We could untie the anchor lines.'

'Float out past the Sunfish Cut, Snake Island, and into the open water.'

'We could look for the steering wheel.'

'We could take the dogs.'

'We could find another island and you could teach me every language you know.'

'Only the dirty words.'

'How do you say *Where is the bordello?* in Finnish?'

'We could invent our own language.'

'Only the dirty words. We could live however we want, Samuel.'

I walk the length of his spine. His skin is bronze next to mine.

'What did you shoot with your arrow?'

'A fox. He was sick. He was going to die too slowly. The hastening of a natural law. Some things cannot last here, Eugenia. It is just too crushing.'

And then, carefully keeping the pages in order, Samuel backtracks. 'I could very calmly go wild.'

'More.'

'I could very calmly go wild.'

In the bath, my blood slows to a sap. I look down at the marks on my skin from my hours with Samuel. They pulse. I hope that he is doing the same. When I watched him gut the fish on a boulder, in the rain, huddled under my suit jacket, making a seam with his thumb, the perch still breathing through its gills, even though its heart jumped in Samuel's palm, I saw that the same life could take place in two locations, and that perhaps this is what love is: the heart of a fish in a palm keeping time with the throbbing body beside it.

I did not tell him where I was going or when I would be back. He will not ask questions until many hours later. He is patient that way. He does not implicate himself in the course of other people's lives. Samuel uses the pay phone by the ferry dock to call his parents on his birthday and theirs. Otherwise, it is impossible to contact him aside from knocking on his door. He does not, living on the water, have an address. He has not had one for a long time. He prefers to land on other people's doorsteps with offerings from his travels: a child's string instrument from Moscow, the best green tea from Yamanashi and, once, a nurse's uniform from a junk shop in Paris. He is good at finding things.

Our last night together, before Samuel finally fell asleep, he showed me a photograph he had taken of a tree beside a Buddhist temple in Kamakura. From it hung prayers, handwritten on slender squares of wood. This is how I feel, crawling into a motel bed in a stranger's nightgown beside a ghost circus, at the other end of this day. Like a tree choked with wishes. I wonder whatever happened to the ordinary moments in the world. To pouring water into a glass, to your feet hitting the floor when you wake up, to the sound of a key in the front door. To thinking that the person across from you will be there the next day and the day after, that your closeness is not an invention but a truth, an unconquerable truth.

Morning creeps in, a grey spectre through the blinds, and I am trying to break the French bread in half. I am hungry. First, I notice the weight of the loaf, and then its refusal to be broken. It is a stubborn bone. I try to break it over the edge of the desk, against the busy walls, the bed frame. I pull at one end and then the other. Clumps of bread fall to the floor and I feel like I am tearing apart prey. I am all urges. *I could very calmly go wild.* I am the bear and when I die, they will find a small hard skull in my stomach.

There is something buried in the loaf's middle. They used to do this in wartime. 'Wives would send their soldier husbands brandy buried in loaves of bread. Mercy is about small gestures,' Cupid told me when she finally woke up, her dog stretching open beside her. It had been three days. Portrait on your easel complete, you stepped away from it and she came to. You cried when she did. Your only magic trick. She chanted, 'Thank you.'

I pull out a bottle and free the cork from it and see, inside, a scroll. I cannot, with my fingertips, pull it out. I run to the receptionist's office. She is still in her blue gown. Her eyes are ringed red. Upon request, she hands me a pair of tweezers – first looking through every drawer in her heavy desk, books teeter-tottering, and then disappearing behind her black curtain, 'I know they're here some somewhere.' The cat that sits by the door has green feathers around his mouth. Last night, in the summer heat, he ate the bird.

The receptionist lets me hold her.

I pull the scroll free from the bottle.

38 Crescentwood Rd.
Scarborough, Ontario

Another map. Hand-drawn perfectly. No asterisks. From here, it is an hour's ride.

I step into my boots and wheel out of the motel room like a daredevil on a motorcycle through a tunnel of fire. My balance is impeccable. It is only halfway that I realize three things: I am still in the stranger's nightgown, flaring silver behind me. Your seat has been adjusted so that my legs can reach the pedals perfectly. And I have never actually pedalled a bicycle before.

I know the receptionist is waving even though I am long out of view. She will remember me as the girl who smelled like love-making. It had been some time.

five

I drop my bicycle and walk the nettled path to the front door. The sun through the willows bleaches the edges of everything. I knock. There is no response. I knock again. Still nothing. Did Finbar die in the night? Have I missed him? I try the handle. The door is unlocked. I push it open and step through. I take in a sharp breath, the long-anticipated moment suddenly real. Instead of the world I imagined, rooms crocheted with spiderwebs, plates stiffened with the remnants of meals, fish skeletons, corks, pits, ashtrays, dog hair, curtains pricked by moths, cluster-fly mounds on windowsills, a house that has not had a woman's touch for too long, it is immaculate. Keys are assembled and hanging from one hook. Shoes are lined up in the front hall. The oak floors are polished. The shoes are too. Persian carpets. Colour-field paintings. The house is a model of propriety. Even ascetic. If Death has been here, he has licked the place clean.

'Hello.' My voice is meek. Barely audible. The chalk of dust in my throat. I catch myself in the hall mirror. I touch my hand to my cheek — a sudden febrility. 'Hello,' I say again, needing to sit down, which I do on the sheen of the floor. Sun thumps in my head. I look back at my footsteps from the front door; they are the tracks of an animal, a stray. I take off my boots and place them on my lap. Spit onto my palm, and rub away at the footprint closest to me. I hear a creaking from the top of the stairwell. I pull myself along the floor to see what it is. There, leaning into the curved banister, standing in elegant repose, is not the man from the photographs — ancient and maimed as I had envisioned him — but a mummy, perfectly, seamlessly wrapped.

You vanished once before. From your adoptive mother, the nurse, Plump Marie Legros Ledoux. A big-pawed scrubber, firm tugs at collars and sleeves, she attended your birth with two other nurses whose faces were much more sour than hers. While you were finding your way into the mortal world, a slender cut at six pounds thirteen ounces, Marie's husband, the maternity-ward doctor, Sheb Ledoux, was picked off the road by black ice. He was not injured, but he was stuck in the ditch. He observed that his eyes were being iced over. He found a pack of matches in his pocket but they were wet and his hands would not work. He started singing a number he saw performed once by a big-breasted bottle-blond burlesquer. He felt impossibly hot. He stripped and was quickly turned white with falling snow.

You were precocious, the nurses all agreed. Most infants are pinched and whining, blind fighters, but you were not. You winked and flirted. Candlelight, soft-shoe, the nurses were thoroughly seduced. Especially Plump Marie who, the next morning, found herself both a widow and a mother.

When you were old enough, you cooked Plump Marie breakfast and left her this note, poor penmanship, always lowercase, on her kitchen table, its brown porcelain top and rust-speckled legs:

> *gone to save the world,*
> *sorry mother,*
> *sorry*
> *yours*
> *sheb wooly ledoux*
> *asshole*

Later that day, Plump Marie was found in her socked feet on her front stoop, staring down the lane, a cob of corn in her right hand, one meagre bite taken, her usual petal-pink lipstick left behind in a smear. French songs about flash-pan loves replayed until they formed bulbs exploding in her head. Veins of white shock collapsed her. In an accident of translation, her obituary listed the cause of death to be failure of the heart.

After you told me this, your stubbled face striped with tears, you left these words in my ear: *Abandonment is a contagion, Eugenia. Abandonment is a curse.*

'You have been unconscious for the better part of a week. So boring for me, my Fata Morgana, when I expected pyrotechnics, but still, welcome, welcome to Orphan Stadium.' Eyes shut, my lids are a pitch against the world. The smell of shaving cream and balsam wax.

'Lucky for me and you – otherwise I would have had another corpse on my conscience – I have some medical know-how.'

I open my eyes and there it is, that spoiled face, moustache sculpted so adroitly across it, his hair, now white, lion-thick and still long to the shoulders. He rubs my right hand, pressing my fingertips between his. He is beautifully assembled in a dark suit and silk tie. The tie is pink and bronze, a column of flowers. A dog pants at his feet like the other end of an obscene phone call. Finbar calls the dog Tulip. I run my left hand over Finbar's cheek. An unfinished encaustic. Before ironing. There is something familiar to it. Not from the photographs, which we studied so closely, but in another sense. It reminds me of the story Samuel told me about a poet lost and frightened in Cairo. Just when she was about to cut her trip short, the Queen streetcar went by – Toronto's old streetcars had been shipped to Egypt. And instantly she was at home. This is how I feel looking at Finbar – he is the Queen car passing me in a strange land.

'You fell in love, didn't you? Ah, the battle.'

I look out the window. Finbar's house is propped up on the Scarborough Bluffs. Toronto Island's raw materials. Made of white sand and clay, the bluffs are built like corrugated castles, the work of extravagant children. In certain early lights, they are copper. Their drops are sheer and if you have vertigo you will swear that, standing still at their edge, you are swaying.

'Did my father come?'

'No.'

'Where did you find his bicycle?'

'His bicycle?'

'The one in the motel room.'

'It was left on my lawn two weeks ago.'

Two nights after he left. The night I tried to hang myself.

'I never did see him, Eugenia. When I noticed the bicycle, I was turning out my lights. It was late. The wheels were still spinning. While I didn't see him, he may have seen me.'

I imagine you in your bare feet shifting in the trees, and Finbar inspecting the dark, 'Who's there?' And you, upon hearing his voice, caving to the ground, for the first time in your life not knowing what to say. Not the reunion you pictured. Not at all.

'When the bicycle was still there in the morning, I thought it might be useful in our correspondence.'

'Why did you send me to the motel? Why did you make me wait?'

'To see if you could.'

I have been here for a week, boxed by a fever in a slender single bed in a spare room with nothing tacked to the walls, a leather chair in one corner where Finbar crossed and uncrossed his legs while reading the newspaper in his fine Italian suits, fresh hydrangea pushed through the buttonhole of his jacket, Tulip's jaw draped over his shoes, both of them, ears tuned to my every breath. 'I did not lie in my biography. I may have exaggerated, which a widower is warranted to do when he wishes for a visitor. I know you expected something much more bilious and decrepit. Sorry to disappoint. Trust me, hand on the faint tick of my heart, Death stalks, and he always has. Even when I was a boy, my relationship with him was a personal one – I had jilted him somehow, cheated, and so he chose me to watch. And yet his preference seems to be for those I love. I come from a long line of suicides. I am constantly trying to redirect his bloodthirst toward the source, but to no avail. You are, Eugenia Ledoux, in some slight danger here, cavorting with the marked likes of me.'

He puts his hand on my forehead. His skin is smooth, the underside of a reptile.

'I am happy you have come. And I am sorry to have startled you into a faint. I dress like that when I go into the city for supplies. I have to say, you startled me too. In the Queen's silver nightgown, you do look so much like her.'

'You have to help me.'

He kisses my forehead, his lips not tingling for the first time in a week. 'You had a high fever, but fire washes us clean, doesn't it.' And then, 'You spoke in your sleep, Eugenia. A language that I do not know. But it reminded me of *La Finta Giardiniera*. My favourite opera. Everyone is mad with love in that opera.'

I stay at Orphan Stadium for the duration of the summer. Finbar and I constellate each other as though we have always been here together under this one sturdy roof. We split a small roast at night. We speak in shorthand. We parcel out the newspaper. We play cards. I wear the Queen's dresses. He hems them for me and handwashes them in the sink. I tell him my middle name. I watch him trim his moustache. By the end, we share our bathwater, and I forget about his face. We do not comment on our likeness; we accept it and recognize its oddity in the unspoken way that twins accept twinship. I tell Finbar about the girl on the rope. I tell him that I want to perform the stunt that no one else can perform. I tell him that you have levitated into outer space, and I imagine you shining in the darkness, a coin in a closed fist, and Finbar says, 'This is something the Queen would believe.' I tell him that I must find you because when I do you will explain everything. You will lay out our history like a set of perfectly tied knots. You will tell me that I did not misinterpret love.

'In order to achieve what it is you wish to achieve, Eugenia, you must make one promise to me now,' he says. 'And it is that while you are here, you will do everything I say.'

Finbar hands me a white shoebox. Inside, wrapped in tissue paper, is a pair of soft leather shoes. Indian leather. Black. 'The only kind to wear.' He ordered them from New York. I slip them on. A second and more intelligent skin. 'It is all in your ankles.' Finbar unlocks the padlock to his basement. He leads me down the narrow stairs. 'Careful.' The room is empty. The walls are covered in knobs. They are made of pine and look like the joints of animals kicking through the cement. They look like Finbar's face. This is his training ground. It has not been touched for thirty-five years. It is the way I imagined his house would be. The dust is upturned urns. I remember Immaculata and me at your funeral. The spatter of rain. Our small hands in the Crock-Pot, felted grey.

'You are in perfect equilibrium only if you can keep your centre of mass over your ankles.' He draws a line between his ribs, extends his arms and, for a moment, is the Vitruvian Man. He has me climb the knobs. Ascend. Descend. Ascend. Descend. I am not allowed to use my hands. I repeat the exercises until I can last long enough, toes tapered into a point, to cook venison soaked in red wine. He chooses venison because it is a tough meat, one that should simmer for a few hours. One that should be marinated for a day if it is to fall succulent from the bone.

'Aside from your ankles, your abdomen will keep you on the rope.' Finbar, in a black three-piece suit, lies on the ground. The posture of a corpse in a casket, and me above, his only mourner. Then he claps the ends of his body together, the jaws of an alligator. A sit-up from a tai chi warm-up, he explains that it will work the muscles buried behind other muscles, the ones that flex in front of my spinal cord. It will make a Roman shield out of my stomach. My turn. He counts as if he were taking my pulse.

Finbar has me lift a barrel over my head, adding an inch of water to it every day until the barrel is full. 'Your arms will stop you from tipping.' Afterwards, hands gripping the barrel's edge, I stretch to strengthen my spine. I grow two inches taller. Finbar lets out the hems of the Queen's dresses.

Always with a sense of ceremony, Finbar ties the braided wire between the willows on his lot. He moves it closer and closer to the edge of the bluffs until I am alongside them; below me, the sad and giant trees, their roots half-exposed, claw the cliffs.

Desperation makes for persistence. I walk with a balancing pole and then Finbar has me drop it over the side of the bluffs. It spears the beach below, the only relic of a very small war. Tulip lunges after it, but Finbar grabs her neck. Her coat in his hand, they look like one creature.

I graduate to the grounds of the nearby Guild Inn. Windows shuttered closed, doors bricked over, the Georgian structure was once a private mansion, then an artist's colony, a World War Two military base and hospital and then a hotel. Now it is full of ghosts. The curious walk its tunnels, plying crucifixes and sprinkling baby powder to track footsteps. They duck between the low pipes, trample the broken tiles, wave away the stench of mildew in the air. Like suitors, they leave gifts — a toy truck and a balloon for the boy once sighted cowering in a corner, one brown eye, one blue. They report whispers in the foyer, the clack of high heels in the upper floors, the squeak of gurney wheels, the shuddering mass of a shell-shocked soldier.

Tulip does not stray as we explore the paths behind the inn, touring the overgrown gardens and winding between the sculptures that stud the landscape: a bronze horse's head, the frontispiece of the Quebec Bank, 'Music Hall' in red sandstone, the entrance to a school for boys. Finbar tells me that these facades were saved from demolished buildings and heritage homes. He knows the details of every one; he remembers when they housed audiences and industry — printing newspapers, readying doctors, hanging thieves. Like Finbar's mind, these decorated onyx and alabaster headstones are a graveyard for the city's architecture.

When I walk the wire between the marble columns of the Greek theatre and the inn, a patchwork of board and brick, swallowing the last of the sun, I hear Tulip growl at the shadows.

At night, I stand in front of the mirror and I trace the new muscles that rise in long strips under my skin. Dorsal fins. Strength is a kind of disfigurement. As a teacher, Finbar is stern and unrelenting. The kindest thing he says to me is, 'History teaches us that the tightrope tends to be a family affair.' He never claps. I fall three times. Three times, he catches me.

One night, Finbar is unwell. I slip into bed with him, the covers on us, heavy like hooked rugs. It is the only time I do this. All my nights are spent in that spare room, replaying the drills of the day, my toughened feet fluttering the sheets, becoming sure as a jungle animal. He says he hears a bell ringing. I hold him from behind. The frailty of his bones. In my arms, he feels breakable. 'Let me tell you about my black armband, Eugenia, my sinkhole, my bullet, my Queen. I would have eaten her toenail clippings for breakfast.' Finbar has never spoken about his Queen. She is an incantation he is ready for only now. 'I howled if she locked the bathroom door. She howled back. This was our ragged cry, our loon song. We chased each other through the halls of this house, spitting on photos of my ancestors — she had none — their grave prohibition faces. We made love for heat or, too tired, too drunk for that, we broke the furniture. *Bonfire the dining room!* she would order. Her eyes: consumption itself. And I would. She made a February night look like the archangel. But she turned my toes to butterflies and pooled me into the most elegant erections the western world has ever seen. God, how I loved her.

'She gets pregnant.' Finbar's voice becomes heavy, brimming with water. 'She does not want to be a mother. She is convinced that she will die young. She always felt this world's grip on her was too weak, too unsure. That it would abandon her. And so she thinks it fit to do it first. She wants the child to be loved. Nine months later, when she starts to feel the faint squirm of pain, we pack our suitcases and we drive. I say choose a direction and she says, "North, go north where the cosmonauts train." She never complains. She changes positions. Leans over the passenger seat. Reclines on her side. But she does not cry once during labour. She is a daughter of pain.

'Twelve hours later, we are in Kapuskasing, Ontario – far enough away from our life that the child will never find us. And the child is coming. We arrive at the hospital. The snow is falling so heavily, the three nurses fear the maternity-ward doctor is stuck in it. One of them is married to him. They will have to deliver the child themselves.

'My Queen checks in under an assumed name. These are the only words she speaks to the nurses. "Rapsodia Satanica." It is the title of an Italian movie. She will not let me come with her. She would let me watch her do most everything else – but not this. I stay in the car until she comes out twenty minutes later, barefoot and in her blue hospital gown. Her toes are painted red. She does not weave when she walks. Always a straight shot. But this night, she is bent forward, heading into a great wind. The snowdrifts are the walls of Troy. It is nearly impossible to get through them. I wrap her in a blanket. She sleeps the whole way home. She has been somewhere she cannot name. She smells like fresh dirt. At one point I pull over and I study her face. Boy or girl? But her face is a wet telegram. Milk fills and hardens her breasts. She wishes it away, and with its drought, the absence of the child becomes too real. Blond like me or dark like her. I beg but she will not tell me anything. She likens it to a death. One she wants to bury. Over the course of the winter, she slowly recovers. That summer, we go to Florence.

'Legend has it that a drunk shook the wire. But this is not true. She had been on my shoulders a hundred times. This was the only time she spoke to me from that height. She said, "You have a son." It was our first walk since his birth. Then she fell. She wanted to.

'She never needed help with her dresses, the way most women do. So tall, she could do all the zippers herself. Whenever we went out, even if it was for an afternoon, she would pack so robustly, as if we would be away for days, for weeks. Her purse was full to bursting with toothbrushes and diaries, underwear, a felt hat, an umbrella. If we flew abroad, she could not sleep the night before for excitement. She sewed drugs into her slippers. She was allergic to everything: ragweed, onions, the cats. But she loved them and did not mind their scratches – even when they ran across her face in the middle of the night. She always had bits of food in her pockets: almonds, bread crumbs, apricots. She was never hungry; she was always starving. We could not have chocolate in the house. If I snuck any in, she would find it, and run to a room she could lock. She would eat all of it in one sitting, not answering me on the other side of the door, not making a sound, until she would emerge, her mouth black like she had broken through the hide of something. She damaged the things she loved because she loved them voraciously. I was always afraid she might snap one of the cats when she held it to her. She did not know her effect. When she danced, she lifted her dress up her thighs. She never looked around to see if anyone was watching. Even though everyone was, she didn't care.

Her world was enough with her in it alone. When she wrote, she wrote furiously. I would ask her what she was working on, she would say, "My eulogy." Children would follow her anywhere. She would half-ignore them and never give them candy, never pinch their cheeks and promise adventure, make faces and voices, shorten their names. She would just continue on and let them observe her. They did not know that for her this was almost an expression of love. She put butter on her eyelashes to make them grow. She sang the wrong words to every song. Even if they knew the right ones, an anthem, a hymn, the children would sing with her. Her version was always better. She rewrote the world around her. She gave everything the incorrect name. Plants, trees, constellations, meats, nuts, seeds – even the children. But no one minded. No one corrected her. Everyone just wanted to hear what they looked like to her. She turned everything into games – games she could never lose. She hated to lose. She could reach cupboards I could not. She never kept anything in its proper place. Wine went under the bed, shoes went above the sink, flowers were planted in the shade. She would stay up all night gardening. I would find her, dress covered in dirt, with a spade. When she did come to bed, she would not wash. In the morning, when she picked up her pastry, her hands were those of a chimney sweep. She asked me for a bugle. I bought her one and she practiced for a year and then put it away carping that she was too old to be the best, why didn't I make her play when she was a girl – though of course we did not know each other then. We met after I walked the Falls the first time. When I opened the door to my hotel room, she was sitting with a dog asleep in her lap. She said it had been following her for days and it told her my room number and that my room number was her future. She said the dog was psychic. When she was pregnant, she would sleep outside our house, under a lean-to she built. She said it was too hot inside. She felt cloistered. She said the child needed air. Once, she climbed on the roof, kicking the ladder away, her belly so full, I screamed at her. When I reached her she said, "You take everything so seriously." She had insomnia. She would wake me up and want to play hide-and-seek through the house. She wanted me to read to her. She loved my voice. She said she loved it so much she wanted to go blind. How she could hear every timbre more sharply if she was blind. She said that when she is gone, to talk, to talk to myself because she would be close and she could listen. To never stop talking. When she slept, her arms would fall over the sides of the bed. She would breathe like an underwater explorer. She never snored. She would tell me her dreams first thing in the morning and then forget them immediately. At lunch I would ask her what she had dreamed about, and she would shake her head. For her, those conversations did not exist. It was too early to be fully alive. If she went for a walk she would go too far and come home with grass and water in her shoes. She could never come through anything without being marked by it. She would fall into black moods and refuse to speak to me for weeks at a time. She would do anything anyone dared her to do — and of a group, she was always the first to drink a homemade wine, to jump from a rock into water, to laugh. No one could keep up. She loved to predict the timing of a storm. When it would hit. She would run to the window, press her forehead against it. A storm was a summons. She was the most interesting person I ever met. The fates, the furies, always leaping between us. She claimed that she chose me for the view. That on a chair on my shoulders, I gave her the best view.

'The only thing she said when she got back into the car that night in Kapuskasing was, "Fuck. My shoes."'

Then Finbar pulls me close, the two of us adrift together. 'It is amazing how alive someone can be in the mind.' It is an instruction. And then, both of us looking straight ahead, 'It is about the bold statements ... ' The prologue to his autobiography.

He makes a ripping sound. Tulip leaves the room.

The next morning, I dig a grave beside the Queen's and I bury Finbar. His face has mended itself through the night. He and the Queen will, in the same violent storm, be pulled into the lake, part of the bluffs' slow collapse. In time, their bones will drift over to Toronto Island and be caught and held by the reeds.

He left one thing for me: a small stack of newspaper clippings. From a distance, they look like your collection of birth announcements. He must have laid them out before dying. His body beside me in the morning. The only body I have been close to that is not breathing. He is holding my hand. He told me that his hand was always steady when he drew maps, but only then. This is how it feels entwined in mine, like it is drawing a map.

A black-and-white photograph of a tree and police crowded beneath it. I make out the faces of the Mime and the Turban, yellow tape across them. *Unidentified Man Found Hanging from Oldest Tree in the Rosedale Ravine.* June 10, 1981. The night I spent on the island. The night I walked the wire for the first time. The second clipping, *Man Found Dead in Ravine Identified as Portraitist Sheb Ledoux.* June 12, 1981. The day Mr. and Mrs. Next Door looked at me with their ruined, clutching faces from amidst the totems of our life, scattered on the lawn like the aftermath of a hurricane. The article details your birthplace, the name of your adoptive mother, the mysterious disappearance of your own mother, your successes as a painter and your time in and out of institutions. It mentions Monique Ledoux, actress and former dancer, your wife of nearly ten years, and your daughters, Immaculata and Eugenia Ledoux. There is a photograph of you.

One I have never seen. Mink must have taken it before we were born. You are planting the apple tree in our backyard.

For Finbar, this was a birth announcement and a death announcement together. It was the first time he had seen a photograph of his son.

If you focus your eyes on one staid object, angle yourself back slightly, jump from a speeding train and land on your feet, you have the sensation of running forty miles an hour. This is how I feel shaking over Finbar's oiled oak table. Grief has its own velocity.

I hope a symphony filled your head.

From here, the city is cells dividing under a microscope. The view from your left eye, floating. The Gardiner Expressway is coiled — a concrete comet, cars hurtling across it, their headlights skidding and stretched white like long exposures. Night is thorough. The moon nearly full, a boulder in a yolk, it shines behind trees, making their branches antlers. Some stars, pricks of silver. The streets are stacked and crooked. Manholes: a cursive of smoke. Leaves, yellow dashes against the pavement. The strut and shuffle of the train across the bridge. Under it, a fold of horns and brakes. Potholes. Chicken and produce trucks drive over them, feathers and skins falling. The raccoons come out. Scurrying, their backs triangles, they walk the edges of fences and rooftops. Pregnant with six at a time. One fox in a park. She barks five syllables and listens for a response. Across a pond that is green and cold. On everything, the white moss of an early frost.

A woman in a knitted hat and dish gloves pulls weeds from a square of dirt with a fork. She tucks seeds into it. A dog skunks by with a bun in his jaw, the mark of lipstick on it. A mezzo-soprano sings. People gather to listen. One has a quail on his head. It lays an egg. Speckled blue. A boy slow-dances. His brother lifts weights beside him. The man gives the egg away. A wet litter of blackbirds is born under a hollow beehive. Small fires in backyards. Leaves in dank piles, burning. The smell of lemon peels and goat. A newborn grabs a fist of his mother's hair. A tooth comes through a gum. A man pushes a shopping cart full of work gloves for sale.

A butcher stops butchering. He wipes his hands down his apron. A congregation on the sidewalk, he joins it. Faces tilted up. Women in caftans, their children a parade behind them, step out onto their porches. A lantern is hung.

Immaculata and Leopold stand on their flat roof. Leopold, his long arm a lance, points up at me. Immaculata holds a white pigeon. The pigeon is so tranquil, I cannot tell if it is alive. The dogs sprint around Immaculata and Leopold in loops, so fast that they become a solid ring. Immaculata looks at them and then Leopold and offers, 'Forever.'

'Forever.'

When they speak, they leave steam, their mouths furnaces. They squeeze their hands together so hard that their fingers hurt. And then Immaculata opens her arms. Unpinned, she is all fluidity. Her dress is a sail. The pigeon flies away. It is a white glove waving.

This is what they all see: a woman walking a wire that is fastened to nothing but the night air. I light my second *REDBIRD* match. My face flickers. It is free the way a nomad's face is free. The match burns out, a twig in my fingertips. One hundred and sixty feet above the city, I am walking Finbar's wire. The one he strung between willows, across the Falls, across Florence. The one that fumbled his Queen. She crushed her heels when she fell. I tell Finbar she tried to land.

A wire memorizes the underside of a foot. How a knife knows a grip. Finbar's wire is broad as the spine of a dinosaur; I walk it vertebra to vertebra. I saw a dinosaur once in the glass case of a museum: a bright green bird with two sets of wings. I tell Mink the bird is her first ancestor. The bird is her beginnings. My heart beats loudly as doors closing behind me. I am not afraid. Every step is a slow and careful assembly. Eyes are remembered and returned to their faces. Portraits are filled in.

Your right eye, the colour of algae, your cheekbones in hard slabs, the sprint of your mouth, your uneven beard. Behind you, a storm. The particles in the air: fingerprint dust. And then, a vast, blue quiet. The lake on the moon. You take off your winter suit. Hang it from a branch nearby. And you swim through water thick as plumage. When you surface, your face is so still, I can make a cast of it.

My hair, your hair, your eyes, my eyes, my face, your face.

Ahead of me, a gold line — the sun prying the horizon open and then in punctures. I am above the lake now, a smooth, wet planet. The city is asleep to the north. 'Find me,' I say and, for a second, the world is empty. 'Find me.' A stamp in the open water, the morning sky behind it an explosion, blackening its shape. You said there was a sandbar in the middle of the ocean. Mustangs galloped across it. You said no one had found it yet, but you wanted me to know it existed. I walk. A man on the roof of his boat. He holds up his hand. There is something in it that catches the light. Around him the waves are hard and grey. The two of us, moving toward each other, making bridges out of space.

Notes and Acknowledgements

The author acknowledges the financial support of the Ontario Arts Council's Chalmers Arts Fellowship and Writer's Reserve Program, the City of Toronto through Toronto Arts Council and the Canada Council.

For temporary residence on islands, thank you to Martin and Gabrielle Alioth, and James Baird of Pouch Cove, Newfoundland; the Gibraltar Point Centre for the Arts, Toronto Island; the National Theatre School, Montreal, Quebec; and especially Ken Gass and the Factory Theatre.

In researching this book, Shane Peacock's *The Great Farini: The High-Wire Life of William Hunt* proved most useful, as did Carole M. Lidgold's *The History of the Guild Inn* and Joanna Kidd's *Nature on the Toronto Islands: An Explorer's Guide.* Thank you also to Sam Sperry, Albert Fulton of the Island Archives, and Jimmy Jones who is the Island archives.

The Guild Inn was still operating in 1981, and there are very few houseboats built from cedar. Immaculata's medieval recipe is abbreviated from Dr. William Kitchiner's *The Cook's Oracle* as cited by Diane Ackerman in *A Natural History of the Senses*. Immaculata's speech to lightning is from S. K. Heninger, Jr.'s *A Handbook of Meteorology* as cited by Annie Dillard in her poem 'A View of Certain Wonderful Effects' in *Mornings Like This*. Samuel and Eugenia's conversation in 3-D glasses begins with a quote from Annie Dillard's *Teaching a Stone to Talk*. On page 160 of the same book, you will find the instructions for jumping from a moving train.

Grateful acknowledgement to the following artists: Chris Cran's 'A Good Boy and a Million Miles of Deep Blue Space'; Veda Hille's 'cowper's folly'; Peter von Tiesenhausen who copyrighted his land as his art; Susan Coolen's *Le Spectacle de la Nature: A Collector's Compendium*, and 'Alien Orbs' from her series *Celestial Travellers*; Max Picard's *The World of Silence*, translated by Stanley Godman; Donna Orchard's *Psycho Killer*; *Paterson Ewen*, edited by Matthew Teitelbaum; aerialist Noah Kenneally; and, for sublime friendship, Heidi Sopinka and Jason Logan.

For belief, thank you to Anne McDermid with Jane Warren, Vanessa Matthews and Martha Magor. To Michael Redhill, Martha Sharpe and Michael Helm, thank you for close reading and esoterica.

Thank you to Alana Wilcox for brilliance. And to Christina Palassio, Evan Munday, Stan Bevington, Rick/Simon and everyone at Coach House Books for making beautiful objects in an elusive address.

Thank you always to the Kerr family, my beloved parents and sister, Sarah. For arriving partway through, thank you to Dove Dey-Kerr.

This book is for Don Kerr, who amazes me.